"Elise Holland's debut novel, *The Thorn Queen,* is a whimsical and deeply satisfying tour de force. The book's plucky heroine, Meylyne, will grab readers by their heartstrings and make them chuckle from page one. There is nowhere readers will rather be than following Meylyne's romp through the richly rendered, otherworldly Glendoch. Meylyne's journey to save her homeland from an evil queen, and her discoveries along the way, will delight and intrigue readers of all ages."

—Andrea Alban, author of *The Happiness Tree* and *Anya's War*

"This middle-grade debut sees a young outcast discover her true potential while on a quest to save others . . . Holland excels in burying twists that flip the whole narrative on its head. Readers should wish for a longer stay in Glendoch. An effervescent fantasy crafted from the heart."

—*Kirkus Reviews*

The Thorn Queen

Elise Holland

Published by SparkPress, a BookSparks imprint,
A division of SparkPoint Studio, LLC
Tempe, Arizona, USA, 85281
www.gosparkpress.com

Published 2018
Printed in the United States of America
ISBN: 978-1-943006-79-3 (pbk)
ISBN: 978-1-943006-80-9 (e-bk)

Library of Congress Control Number: 2018937853

Book design by Stacey Aaronson

Perched in a sprawling Orange Willow, she wedged herself between two branches and looked down.

1

A Broken Rule

THERE WAS NO DOUBT THAT MEYLYNE HAD THE BEST seat in the house. Perched in a sprawling Orange Willow, she wedged herself between two branches and looked down. Tyr's town square had never looked so crowded. Hundreds of people jostled and shouted beneath her.

"Is the entire Above-World here?" she whispered.

"Yes," the tree whispered back. "Prince Piam only visits once a year."

Meylyne blinked in surprise. Not because the tree had spoken to her—she was used to that—but because she hadn't realized the prince was so private. Brightly colored scarves and jewels flashed in the sunlight while peddlers' carts rocked within the flood of people. The smell of kettle-corn and nutmeg wafted up to her and she leaned forward for a better view.

"No way will everyone fit. You can barely squeeze the Tyrians into their town square—let alone all the *other* Above-Worldians too!"

The tree's twigs jabbed at Meylyne's arms and face, forcing her back into the shadows of its branches.

"Ow! Stop it," she protested.

"Well get out of sight! You aren't allowed in the Above-

World—you're trespassing here. You know what'll happen if you get caught!"

The Shadow Cellars, Meylyne thought. Dank dungeons full of bones and worms and vengeful ghosts. And the tree would get the axe if the royals knew it had helped hide her. She pulled a large orange blossom in front of her. The tree was right. No sense in taking chances.

More and more people swarmed into the square. Just as Tyr was bigger than its neighboring cities, its inhabitants were on the bigger side too. The Tyrians stood in clumps, looking large and faintly orange-hued from the dust of the Orange Willows while the others climbed on the benches and tables, hoisting their children with them. Some even spilled into the icy-cold pond. Here and there, small skirmishes broke out between the Tyrians and their neighbors. A small boy, perched on his father's shoulders, spat shaved ice through his straw at a canary cage hanging from a bird-seller's cart.

"Knock it off or I'll put you in a cage!" the bird-seller roared.

"My bonnet!" another voice howled. "You're trampling my new bonnet, you buffoon!"

Meylyne giggled as she spotted the hatless victim—a very skinny lady with her hands clamped to her head.

Weedy little thing. I bet she's a Welkan.

Welke was one of the cities directly bordering Tyr and its plants-only diet left the Welkans with a greenish pallor. A man bent over to pick up the lady's hat, knocking into at least three others with his big bottom. Even more people yelled at him.

"Don't you shout at my husband," a woman bellowed. "This is our town square—you Welkans can clear off!"

The father of the ice-spitting boy set down his son, his

face red and radish-like with rage as he advanced upon the big-bottomed Tyrian man. On his tip-toes he was half the larger man's size. Meylyne gasped as he head-butted the colossal Tyrian in the stomach, presumably because that was all he could reach. The Tyrian stumbled backward, righted himself and then thumped the Welkan's head. Within seconds, two town sentinels dashed over, brandishing their swords and whisked away the offenders. Everyone moved apart, hissing at one another like a bunch of bad-tempered cats.

"It's dreadful," the tree tutted. "The Above-World used to live in harmony. Now you'd think the Tyrians and Welkans hated each other."

"Yes, terrible," Meylyne replied, although secretly she had found the whole spectacle more entertaining than upsetting. A bronze-skinned peddler caught her attention as he weaved deftly through the crowd. Fragments of his cries floated up to her.

". . . silks from Ka-Ffyr . . . spiced apples, three for a penny . . ."

"I'd give anything for an apple," she murmured.

"Don't even think about going down there," the tree replied. "You stay where you are—"

The tree's words were drowned out as someone boomed through a megaphone—

"MAKE WAY! MAKE WAY! HERE COMES PRINCE PIAM!"

The crowd parted to let through a line of guards mounted on white horses. All wore the Cardinal House uniform—black feathered helmets, gold-and-turquoise suits, and shiny black boots. The horses' manes were braided with gold ribbons and bells jangled around their ankles. Meylyne felt the usual combination of awe and disdain at the sight of them.

Thirteen guards. Those tall orange-faced ones must be Tyrians. The little sprouty one's a Welkan. She squinted at the others. They were further back and harder to make out. One of the guards looked toward her and she ducked back behind the branches. After a few seconds, she peeped out.

He was still looking at her.

Her palms began to sweat. Counting to ten, she peeped out again and her whole body sagged in relief.

Phew. He's gone!

"That was far too close," the tree reproached her, trembling. "I'm shaking in my roots! What if he had suspected something?"

Meylyne swallowed. Trespassing in the Above-World really was the stupidest thing she had ever done. Well, not so much the trespassing—it was the hanging around part that was stupid. After all, she'd got what she came for. Reaching into her pocket, her fingers closed around a small, hard object.

Mother won't believe it when she sees what I found for her.

Picturing the look of happiness and admiration on her mother's face, a warm glow swelled inside her, squelching the remorse she had felt just seconds earlier. She could stay a few extra minutes to see Prince Piam. No one would notice her. She was too small to be mistaken for a Tyrian and too big for a Welkan, but with her long black hair and pasty complexion she could easily pass for a merchant's daughter from Mirym.

"Don't worry. I swear I'll go home the minute I've seen Prince—"

Meylyne's mouth snapped shut as a squat, roundish lady crawled up next to her. Pink-faced and puffing, she looked around and then stared at Meylyne. "Who are you talking to? Shift over, dearie, there's room for two up 'ere."

"I don't like her," the tree whispered.

Meylyne studied the lady as she ogled the crowd. She obviously hadn't heard the tree. Not that that surprised her. Apart from her father, Meylyne was the only Hearer left that she knew. The lady's jowl hung down from her chin to the base of her neck and wobbled violently as she waved her arms in the air, squealing, "I think I see 'im!"

The branch beneath them swung from side to side, tipping Meylyne out of her nook. She grabbed hold of the branch above her.

"Oops—sorry dearie!" the lady apologized, grabbing the back of Meylyne's cape. "Didn't mean to do that." She gave Meylyne a quick once over. "What've you got underneath that cape? You look more like a big black crow than a little girl!"

And you look like a big pink iguana.

"Get away from her," the tree urged. "She's trouble."

The lady squealed again. "Oh look! It *is* 'im!"

"Move back," the tree hissed. "Now!"

Meylyne bit her lip. *If I move back now, I'll miss my chance to see Prince Piam.*

"In a second," she murmured.

Crouching down next to the lady, Meylyne ignored the tree's sighs as another procession trotted into the square. It was led by a boy with blond, shoulder-length hair and skin the color of sand from the Drylands and although he wore the same uniform as the guards, he was clearly not a guard.

Sitting very straight on his beautiful palomino mare, he smiled and waved at the people around him.

The lady elbowed Meylyne.

"You can tell he's a Cardinal, can't you? Look at them big brown eyes and dimples. Ooo but he 'as grown. I saw 'im last year and 'e was 'alf his size then! He looks to be twelve now."

Yes, Meylyne thought, her eyes riveted on the prince. *He does look about my age. But so ordinary. You'd think with his disease and being a Cardinal prince and all, he'd look a bit different.*

"He's coming right this way!" the lady wheezed. "Oh but he's a scruffy one. Look at his hair all uncombed like that! Merciful heavens, he's comin' right underneath us—Prince Piam . . . *Prince Piam!*"

Leaning over the branch, the lady stretched a pudgy hand toward the Prince, shoving Meylyne to the side as she did so. There was a loud snap as one of the branches broke.

"Whoa!" Meylyne cried, grabbing at some twigs above her. They came away in her fingers. Everything next was a blur as terror like electricity jolted through her . . . *world tilting ... stomach lurching ... lady thrusting out her hand ... fingertips brushing ...*

"Aaaaaaaahhhhhhhhhh!!!"

Meylyne plummeted toward the prince. His head snapped up and he grunted like a hog as she hit him square in the chest. Together they thudded to the ground. The prince cushioned her fall but still the world swam and she tasted blood and ice in her mouth. Struggling to breathe, she was dimly aware of flailing hooves and a blur of guards grabbing the reins, pulling the terrified animal away. Other guards dropped to the prince's side.

"Are you alright, sir?" one guard asked. Another grabbed Meylyne's cloak. In a flash, she was on all fours. Scooting backward, she twisted out of his grasp.

"Oy—you! Come back here!"

Meylyne scrambled into a thick ring of ferns bordering the pond. The dense leaves instantly swallowed her up. The guard made as if to follow her.

"Leave her," another guard cried. "The prince is looking like puddled milk. We have to get him back to the palace, sharp-like!"

"Heavens, you're right! Come on then, let's get him on his horse. You lot—find that girl!"

Meylyne heard the guards wheeze as they heaved the prince onto his horse and then hooves clattering as they charged out of the square. Others began poking their swords into the ferns. Meylyne gasped as a sword grazed her chin. On her hands and knees, she scuttled around to the other side of the pond as fast as she could and peered out. A mass of legs ran this way and that. She waited for a break in the traffic and then sprang into it. Pushing her way forward, she caught flashes of steel through the people crisscrossing before her. She was on the other side of the square—the entrance not far away.

"Keep walking," she muttered to herself. "You're almost at the gates. Just a few feet more . . . oh no!"

Guards stood on either side of the gates. One looked straight at her and she ducked into a tea-house. It was dark inside, with no one behind the counter. The armchairs and tables were empty too. A smell of orange and cardamom wafted from a pot, hanging over a fire. As Meylyne sped toward the latrines in the back, she heard someone enter behind her.

"I know you're in here," a voice warned. "Come out and there'll be no trouble."

Meylyne ran into one of the stalls and locked the door behind her. There was a small window above one of the clay commodes, just big enough for her to squeeze through.

Please, please, please be open.

She climbed upon the commode and pushed the window. It didn't budge. An old latch held it at the top. While she struggled with it, the door to the latrines opened and slammed shut. Footsteps thudded toward her stall. The door handle jiggled.

"Open up at once!"

Meylyne set her eyes on the latch. "*Vagabotch!*" she hissed.

The latch began to swell and Meylyne ducked as it burst, shards of rusty metal clattering into the walls around her.

The door handle stopped jiggling and the voice came again. Now it sounded alarmed.

"What's going on?"

Great. Meylyne groaned inwardly. *Just add unauthorized use of alchemy to my list of crimes.*

The latch was supposed to have melted quietly, but as usual she'd got the incantation wrong. Hoisting herself up onto the windowsill, she looked down. The street below was empty. A short drop to the ground and she was free.

There was a crash and the door to her stall flew open. A voice roared behind her.

"Hey—stop!"

Meylyne felt a hand brush the back of her cloak as she

jumped. She landed on her hands and knees, got her bearings, and then dashed into a deserted side street. A few feet away, a grate rusted in the ground. Within seconds she was on her haunches, grunting as she heaved it aside. A set of rungs led down below. Lowering herself into the hole, she clung on with one hand and gritted her teeth as she pushed back the grate with the other. It slowly scraped into place.

Meylyne leaned her forehead against a rung. She knew the guard wouldn't follow her into the Between-World—trespassing in another world was far too serious an offence. She enjoyed a fleeting sensation of relief before the horrible truth sank in.

And that's not even the worst thing I did today!

2

Facing the Music

As Meylyne climbed down the ladder, she began to shake uncontrollably. In one day she had managed to break two of Glendoch's First Rules—trespassing in the Above-World and doing sorcery without permission. And, far worse, she'd squashed Prince Piam!

If only I'd listened to the tree when—

"Pssst!"

Meylyne's head jerked up. To her right was a cave and peering from one of the upstairs windows was her friend Trin. He looked like a boy in a bird suit, but in fact his feathers and beak were real. Trin was a garlysle—a native of the Between-World.

"Meylyne! What the—?"

He trailed off as he got a good look at her. Her hair was full of leaves, she had a bloody chin, and her cloak was torn.

"Stay there. I'll be right down."

A few minutes later, Trin hurried from his cave. His red-gold feathers were lying flat and looked damp, like he had just had a bath.

"What happened to you?"

He glanced up at the grate and then back at Meylyne.

"Tell me you weren't in the—" he lowered his voice. "Above-World!"

Meylyne nodded. The look on Trin's face was so awful that for a second she was afraid she might cry. Trin grabbed her wrist and pulled her around to the side of his cave, out of sight. Although they were the same age, he had about three feet on her.

"What? *Why?* You know you're not allowed up there, even if you are half-human!"

Her chin wobbling, Meylyne gave Trin an impatient look. He was one of the most intelligent garlysles she knew but he said the most obvious things at times.

"Of course I know that." She took a deep breath. "I did it so I could find my mother's opal—"

"And that's another thing," Trin interrupted. His expression was grave. "Your mother's looking for you."

"*No!* She was supposed to have been gone all day. Does she know I was in the Above-World?"

Now it was Trin's turn to give her an impatient look.

"Your mother is Glendoch's most powerful alchemist. I'm sure she knows! You'd better get home right now—and I mean *right now*." He peered over his shoulder. "If she catches us chatting, she'll turn me into a speckled slug. Try to come over later. We'll wait up for you."

By "we" he meant himself and his twin, Train. They were Meylyne's best friends. In fact, her *only* friends. None of the other garlysles wanted anything to do with her, what with her scary mother and even scarier father. He gave her a quick hug and sped back inside his cave.

Fingering the tear in her cloak, Meylyne's mind scrambled

for excuses. She gave up. In no way were trespassing and flattening the Prince excusable.

As she trudged down the maze of red clay tunnels leading to her cave, beads of sweat gathered on her forehead and she shrugged off her cloak. Colorful rugs, talon-crafted by the garlysles, decorated the walls but Meylyne paid no attention to these right now.

She felt sick at the thought of what she'd done.

All too soon, she entered into her tunnel. Her footsteps slowed down as she approached her cave. Great-Uncle Groq lived just a few doors down.

Forget about Mother. He'll be ten times worse when he finds—

She jumped as her front door burst open. Her mother glowered down at Meylyne, lancing her with her ice-pick eyes, her raven-black hair coiled on top of her head like a serpent ready to strike. A blue vein pulsed in her temple.

Meylyne swallowed.

"H-hello Mother. I—"

"Not a word," her mother hissed. Seizing her arm, she dragged Meylyne inside their cave, slamming the door behind them. The small, stark living room looked just as Meylyne had left it. A sagging brown couch slumped in the middle of the room, spilling its insides on the uncarpeted floor from a tear that her mother had never bothered to fix. A cardboard box served as a coffee table. A single painting hung on the wall opposite—a garish jumble of lines that looked like two birds pecking the eyes out of a fish.

"Sit," her mother ordered, pushing Meylyne toward the couch. "What do you have to say for yourself?"

Meylyne hung her head.

"I-I'm sorry, Mother."

"Sorry for what? Trespassing in the Above-World or falling on the prince?"

Meylyne felt herself flush. As usual, her mother knew everything.

"Both."

Her mother clenched her hands, her already pale skin turning a grayish shade of white. "For goodness sake, Meylyne, when Groq gets wind of this, he'll show no mercy. Family or not!"

An icy finger crept up Meylyne's spine. As luck would have it, Meylyne's Great-Uncle Groq was also the Prime Minister of the Between-World. He was the opposite of lenient. Meylyne spent most of her time trying to be invisible to him, which was not hard as he seemed equally determined to ignore her.

"I know Mother. I swear I never thought I'd get caught. I look just like an Above-Worldian!"

Her mother's face twisted with such anger that Meylyne wished she could bite back the words. "As if that's an excuse for breaking the rules. You may be part-human but you're still a Between-Worldian. Why, *why* did you go up there?"

Meylyne looked down at the ground. Her plan had gone so horribly wrong. She felt her throat tighten.

"I went to find your black opal," she mumbled.

For a moment her mother looked perplexed. Then she shook her head. "How did you know about that?"

Meylyne blinked away the tears filling up her eyes.

"I overheard you and Great-Uncle the other night. You said you had lost it. I know how much you love it, so I asked the Well if it knew where your opal was—"

"What?" her mother interrupted. "You asked who?"

"The Wise Well of M'Yhr."

Her mother raised an eyebrow. "Oh, so the Well is talking to you now, is it?"

Meylyne nodded. "Uh-huh. Anyway—it said your opal was in the stream between Tyr and Welke. I wasn't going to go, but then I woke up this morning and it was like I just *had* to. I figured there was no way I'd get caught—you were supposed to be gone all d—"

She bit her lip. She hadn't meant to admit that last bit.

"Go on," her mother replied, crossing her arms.

"Yes. Sorry." Meylyne's words started to tumble over one another. "I snuck out through the west grate and went to the stream which was just where Well said it would be and then the stream told me where to look and, and, I did it — I found your opal!"

She reached inside her pocket and drew out a greenish-black stone. Her mother took the stone from her hand, her expression softening as she closed her fingers around it.

"Then what happened?"

Meylyne's shoulders sagged. No "thank you" or anything. That was supposed to have been the part where her mother had showered her with admiration and love. Maybe even looked happy for once.

"Then two people walked by, talking about how Prince Piam was coming out for one of his yearly visits to Tyr's town square. I *had* to see him . . . I figured it was the only chance I'd have and I'd heard so much about him, what with that weird disease he was born with and all."

She drew a breath, aware she was babbling again. "So I

went to Tyr and hid in a tree . . . but then this stupid woman knocked me out of it right as he was passing by underneath and I fell on him."

At the memory of this her face crumpled. She looked down at the ground so that her mother wouldn't see her cry. Her mother couldn't abide sniveling.

"I'm sorry Mother."

Her mother's eyes blazed. "As well you should be. I know you meant to do the right thing but this ... this is a catastrophe." She drew a deep breath. "Did anyone recognize you?"

Meylyne wiped her eyes.

"Who would recognize me? No one knows me up there, and I don't look like *him.*"

Meylyne cringed the minute she said it. *Him* was her garlysle father, Meph. He had left to pursue a life of crime the day she was born. Not a welcome subject in her home—or anyone's for that matter.

Her mother turned her back on her. "I must have dropped my opal the last time I was out hunting for him. Fetch me my crystal."

Sliding off the couch, Meylyne trudged into her mother's bedroom. On one side of the room was a mattress covered with a gray blanket. Opposite was a wooden dresser with a jewelry box on it. She reached behind her mother's only piece of jewelry—a finely-spun rose-gold necklace—and pulled out an oddly-shaped piece of glass. Curved on one side and straight on the other, it was about the size of a text book and looked like a fragment of something larger. She returned to the living room and handed it to her mother.

Sitting down, Meylyne's mother tapped the crystal and

whispered. Meylyne watched over her shoulder as images swirled on the glass.

"Meylyne stop hovering. Go and sit down over there—out of my sight."

Meylyne retreated to the corner. "Can't I just—"

"Sit!"

Meylyne sat in the corner. If only she had stayed in bed that morning. She wiped her nose. Well, maybe she would've still snuck out but she'd have come *straight* home after getting the opal.

Five minutes passed. It felt more like five hours. As Meylyne watched her mother frown at the crystal, a memory popped into her mind. In it, she was just a little girl, allowed to look in the crystal for the first time. She had held her breath as a world of white ice, blue skies, and flowers that sparkled like jewels appeared in the glass.

"See. Glendoch is a glacier," her mother had said. "A gigantic ice-island."

A glacier. Meylyne had hungrily taken in the crooked buildings, parks, and trees that seemed to grow willy-nilly wherever they chose. But most of all, it was the Above-Worldians who captured her attention. A whole country of people that looked like she and her mother looked, with smooth skin, no beaks, no feathers … and their *clothes!* Meylyne had grown up in a brown pinafore, and looked upon their multicolored suits with awe.

"There are so many of them," she had whispered to her mother.

"Yes," her mother said, "more of them than there are garlysles down here."

"Then why are we down here instead of up there with them?"

"Because you are part-garlysle. They wouldn't have us up above."

The memory faded. Although Meylyne could only see the side of her mother's face, it seemed like her frown was getting worse.

Meylyne's insides tightened. It was her fault her mother frowned so much. How could Glendoch's most powerful sorceress be happy when her only daughter was an alchemical dunce? Meylyne felt like a gnat most of the time, buzzing around her mother's head.

A tear plopped out of her eye. Better a gnat than *this*.

Finally her mother put down the crystal.

"Well?" Meylyne asked. "What did you see?"

Her mother gave her a long look. "It appears that you were recognized after all."

Meylyne gaped at her mother. "But—"

"Yes," her mother went on. "Right now, Queen Emery and her ghastly sage are discussing what ought to be done about it."

She stood up.

"Stay here. I must speak with your Great-Uncle. At least I am spared the task of punishing you," she added, more to herself than to Meylyne. "That which lies ahead of you is far worse than anything *I* could have thought up."

3

What the Well Said

MEYLYNE STARED AFTER HER MOTHER IN DISBELIEF. Dread settled inside her like mud in the pit of her stomach.

How could I possibly have been recognized? No one knows me up there. Mother must be mistaken.

She chewed her nails. Her mother was Glendoch's most powerful sorceress. She was never mistaken. Jumping to her feet, Meylyne dashed out of the living room, through the kitchen and into the pantry. A stack of cauldrons stood against the far wall. Pushing them aside, she crouched down and pressed her ear up to the wall. Her great-uncle's study was on the other side. After a minute, she heard voices approaching.

"Sit," one of the voices barked. It was her great-uncle. "What is it, Ellenyr?"

Meylyne heard her mother murmuring in reply. Rich and velvety, there was no mistaking her voice.

"Meylyne did what?" her great-uncle roared.

More murmuring from her mother. A bead of sweat trickled down Meylyne's face.

"No," she heard her great-uncle groan. "They're going to demand *what?*"

Meylyne grew hot, then cold all over.

"I can just see what's going through the royals' minds. Meylyne is Meph's daughter. They will say she is just like him—born to do nothing but terrorize their citizens." He paused and Meylyne pictured him clutching his head with his talons. "I just don't understand it," he went on. "Meylyne has always been so quiet —so *obedient* before now!"

Meylyne's mother murmured again.

"Your opal?" Now her great-uncle sounded more incredulous than angry.

Her mother said something in reply and for a minute there was silence.

"Well, I suppose that counts for something," her great-uncle said at last. "Not to the royals, mind you. They won't care about your opal at all. All they shall want is to turn this situation to their advantage, which means that you must do as they say. I suppose we should at least try to reason with them and we might as well go now. The queen is easiest to deal with at this time of day while she partakes of her wine."

Meylyne heard a door close and then everything became quiet. Pushing herself to her feet, she traipsed back into the living room and mulled over what she'd just overheard. She didn't like the sound of her mother having to "do what they said."

I wish I could see the Well right now. I bet it would know what that meant.

She gnawed on her nails again. Her mother had told her to stay there.

Oh she'll be gone at least an hour—I'll be back long before that!

Jumping up, she ran outside and hurried down the lane,

turning toward the town center. Here, the caves nestled closer together and in the distance she saw garlysles strutting in and out of shops and cafes. The sound of a flute floated toward her. As she passed by a bakery, a smell of ginger wafted out through an open window. Two garlysles sat with their backs to her, drinking ginger-nog at the counter. They turned as she walked past. One nudged the other and whispered to her friend.

Meylyne ignored them. She was used to the stares by now. They were all part and parcel of being the daughter of the Between-World's most notorious garlysle, and its most brilliant sorceress. Not to mention being the Prime Minister's great-niece. Turning right at the next corner, she left the bustle of the town center and headed toward the old dye-making district. The tunnel widened, glowing red and green from the minerals in the clay, and the sounds of the town faded to silence.

No one came to this part of the Between-World any more. The old, derelict dye makers' caves were all shuttered up; their abandoned machinery cracked and rusted. Behind them was a mound of earth known as Thingummy and to its right a deep basin—the Old Well of M'Yhr.

No one called the Between-World "M'Yhr" any more either. But as the Between-World's oldest structure, the Well had been allowed to retain its original name. The Well's waters used to have healing powers, but if they still did, no one knew. The healers had long since stopped using them, preferring to buy potions from the Above-World instead.

Kneeling at the Well's edge, Meylyne splashed her hand in the ruby-red water. A voice emerged, sweet and melodic like a choir singing.

"What ails thee, child?"

Her voice cracking, Meylyne explained all that had happened and what she had overheard between her great-uncle and her mother. "They're with the royals now," she finished dramatically, "probably bargaining for my life!"

"There is no sense in that." The Well sighed. "The Above-World is in turmoil. Queen Emery will have to deal you the worst punishment, or seem weak before her people."

Meylyne felt like a giant hand was inside her chest, squeezing her heart.

"What should I do?"

"You must flee."

"Flee?" Meylyne cried. "Where to? There's nowhere in the Between-World that I can hide and I can't possibly go above-ground again!"

"Indeed that is where you must go—back to the stream in which you found your mother's opal. There you will find a dappled gray stalliynx. Tell him you need safe passage to the Valley of Half-Light—"

Meylyne gasped. "The Valley of Half-Light?" She dropped her voice to a whisper. "I'm not going there!"

"Yes, you are, for it is there that you shall find the cure for Prince Piam's rapid-aging disease and *you* must cure him. It is the only way. This is your fate, Meylyne."

"My fate? What are you talking about?"

"You wish for your mother to be proud of you, do you not? You wish for the garlysles to see you as something other than the daughter of an outlaw and a sorceress, or as the Prime Minister's great-niece."

"Of course I do."

"Then do not argue with me. This is your fate I tell you."

"But . . . but the Valley of Half-Light is where the sphers live." Meylyne's voice became hoarse. "They eat souls."

"Oh the sphers can be kept at bay with the right incantation." The Well's voice became mournful. "But you must go now, before your mother returns home. Take her crystal so she cannot track you. Take your Book of Enchantments too. You must improve your alchemical skills by far."

Meylyne sat back on her heels. "But—"

The Well's water rose up, spraying her. "No more arguments. Go. *Now.*"

Meylyne pushed herself to her feet and ran back the way she had come. Once home, she began to pace across the living room, thoughts whirling around her mind.

The Well must be crazy! No way am I going to the Valley of Half-Light. No one has ever come out of there alive!

She plopped down on the couch and clutched her head. The Well was anything but crazy—it had never steered her wrong yet.

If only I knew what was going on at the Castle. Maybe things aren't as bad as I thought.

Glancing down to her right, she found her mother's crystal where she had left it. Meylyne had been told never to look in it without her mother's supervision. Licking her lips, she picked it up and tapped it, murmuring the word she had heard her mother say a thousand times before. "*Ostendee.*"

Colors swirled in the glass, blurring her reflection. "Show me Glendoch Castle."

A beautiful, three-winged castle emerged through the swirling colors. Built from the Glendochian mineral oremin, its pale green walls cast a soft glow in the evening sun. Rose-gold tiles sparkled throughout the roof.

"Visitors chambers," she added.

A room flickered into view. Red brocade covered the walls. In the center of the room, an assortment of plush chairs surrounded a glass table. Meylyne's mother and great-uncle perched on two of the chairs. Queen Emery was directly across from them.

Even sitting down, she looked very tall. Her long red hair was swept up into braids coiled around her head and she wore a long, white, satin gown. Next to her sat a short, hedgehoggy-looking man. This was Chifflin, her sage. Both he and the queen frowned while her great-uncle spoke.

"We understand that she has broken a First Rule and should be subject to the maximum punishment. I feel just as strongly as you that we need to keep our worlds separate. We cannot return to a state of war. But you must leave Meylyne's father out of this."

Meylyne's shoulders sagged. Things never boded well for her when her father entered the conversation.

"I know he causes your queendom great distress," her great-uncle went on, "but you cannot blame Meylyne for his deeds."

"Can't I?" Queen Emery replied. There was a razor-sharp edge in her voice. "How am I to know that she is not allied with her treasonous father?" She paused to sip from her silver goblet. "It does not help that she is regarded as an abomination by most of my queendom." She shot Meylyne's mother a cold stare. "Our worlds are not meant to interbreed."

Meylyne's mother met the queen's gaze. "Respectfully, I disagree."

Meylyne held her breath. Her great-uncle could get away with saying that—he was the queen's equal. Her mother was not. The queen's eyes blazed but her mother did not look away. Meylyne suspected that this was why Queen Emery hated her mother so much—her icy indifference.

Meylyne knew first-hand how *that* felt.

Chifflin cleared his throat.

"It is just that we have a delicate situation here, Prime Minister Groq. As you know, the troubles that Meph—your *nephew"*—Meylyne's great-uncle stiffened as Chifflin stressed the family tie—"heaps upon us divide our Queendom more and more every day and our citizens blame us for our inability to protect them. The memory of the Cabbage-Wind haunts us all still."

"Some of us more than others," Meylyne's mother replied, her voice steely. "You know I search for Meph constantly. Last time I came close." She held up her arm to reveal a curved scar. "One of these days, I will catch my husband and bring him to justice."

"Yes. One day." Queen Emery took another sip of wine. "In the meantime, I see an opportunity here."

Meylyne's mother sat back and sighed.

"You want me to cure Prince Piam of his rapid-aging disease."

Queen Emery smiled. "How astute of you. It is a perfect solution, is it not? This way, you prove your loyalty to us and we pardon Meylyne. We all win."

"We have tried this before, with disastrous results," Meylyne's mother replied. "My sorcery cannot cure him. Your doctors cannot cure him. Your explorers have died, in search of his cure—"

"Regardless of all that, you *must* cure him!"

Meylyne flinched as Queen Emery slammed her goblet down on the table. Wine splashed everywhere.

"Look at the state of my Queendom! You speak of war between our worlds? Well war *within* my world is near! Half of my queendom has lost faith in me. I need to show them that I am not some pathetic, cursed being—incapable of protecting them against a rogue garlysle, or giving them a healthy heir to the throne . . ."

Queen Emery fell silent while a servant dabbed a cloth into her spilled wine. As soon as the servant had left, a bell sounded in the distance.

"You know that it will take more than Prince Piam's good health to restore your people's faith in you," Groq said.

"Perhaps. Perhaps not." Queen Emery drained the rest of her wine. "Either way, it is time to conclude this meeting. Are we clear on my terms?"

"Yes," said Meylyne's mother. "You will pardon Meylyne as long as I cure Prince Piam."

"Correct. Of course I shall have to imprison Meylyne in the Shadow Cellars in the meantime. I can't have my people think I am entirely addle-pated. You have three months to find or conjure up my son's cure. If you fail, I shall have to send Meylyne to the Snake People. It was, after all, a First Rule that she broke."

The crystal slid from Meylyne's knees.

The Shadow Cellars ... and then the Beneath-World?

The floor tilted beneath her and for a second she thought

she would be sick. Images of everything she had ever known about the Beneath-World flashed through her mind—the scorching mud, the streams of fire and, worst of all, the Snake People. Hateful creatures with human bodies and snake heads.

She stood up. The Well had been right about everything, and this meant one thing.

I have to run away!

4

Hope

DASHING TO HER BEDROOM, MEYLYNE GRABBED HER rucksack. Her eyes darted around the room as she began throwing things into it.

Spell book, quilt, medicine ... what else?

She hurried back into the living room and almost tripped over her mother's crystal. At first she just stared at it. Her mother would be beside herself when she found it gone—probably even more so than finding her *daughter* gone.

You have to take it—the Well said so.

She pushed the crystal into her rucksack. *I'll leave her a note,* she thought, running into the kitchen. *Then she'll know why I've run away, and I'll promise to take care of her crystal.*

She filled a drinking-pouch with water and squashed it into her bag along with some daffy-seeds, a loaf of bread and a packet of figs. She realized that she had slopped half of the water over her pinafore and dabbed at it with a towel. There was no time to change. Her mother would be home at any minute. Hoisting her bulging rucksack onto her back, she grabbed her cloak and sped outside.

As she neared the town center, she found the usual throng of garlysles milling about; picking up their groceries for supper or taking their children to pottery class. Everything looked so ordinary that tears pricked her eyes. She would give anything for her life to go back to normal.

Fat chance of that, she thought bitterly. *In a few minutes, my mother will read my note and—*

She gasped and stopped so suddenly that a garlysle bumped into her from behind.

I forgot to leave a note!

The garlysle grumbled at her.

"Oh just go around me," she snapped.

The garlysle looked outraged but moved away as she began muttering to herself.

"I am *such* an idiot. Now what am I supposed to do? I can't just run away without leaving a note!"

An idea clicked in her mind. She dashed off in the opposite direction and did not stop running until she had reached Trin and Train's cave. She banged on the door.

"Come *on,*" she muttered.

The door opened and her friend Train peeped around it. Aside from her feathers being longer around her face, she looked identical to Trin. Her beak widened into a huge grin.

"*Meylyne!* What are you doing here? I thought you'd be shut in forever . . ."

Meylyne quickly stepped inside, shutting the door behind her. "Train, shush! I'm sorry but I don't have much time. Where's Trin?"

"Here."

Trin walked up behind them. Grasping their talons, Meylyne pulled them into their room. Two nests were perfectly made up against the far wall. Meylyne sat in one of them and Trin sat in the other. Train squeezed in next to her.

"Well?" Train demanded.

Meylyne's chin wobbled. "It's really bad. I have to go back into the Above-World."

"*What?* You're kidding right?" Train spluttered.

"I wish!"

Meylyne rushed to explain everything as quickly as possible.

". . . so now Queen Emery's really mad and saying I'm in cahoots with my father," she finished. "She's insisting that my mother prove our loyalty by curing Prince Piam of his disease or I'll get sent to the Beneath-World."

Trin's and Train's feathers clamped down on their backs. They looked as if water had been poured over them.

"Oh Meylyne, you never should have gone in the Above-World. Your mother would've lived without her stupid opal!"

Meylyne wiped her face. Train was right. She was an idiot to have expected her mother to be proud of her just because of that.

"And Queen Emery is such a beast. Everyone knows there's no cure for Prince Piam's weird aging disease," Train continued.

"Well here's the worst part," Meylyne replied. "According to the old Well of M'Yhr, there is a cure and *I'm* the one that has to get it. That's why I have to go to the Above-World again—it's where the cure is."

Trin and Train gaped at her.

"I know it sounds crazy, but the Well wouldn't lie."

"No, but what about your mother?" Train asked. "She'll come looking for you, and you'll be in double the trouble when she catches you!"

"She won't find me. She has no idea where I'm going."

Meylyne cleared her throat. "Which is why I need you to give her a message."

Trin and Train recoiled. They were terrified of Meylyne's mother.

"What message?" asked Trin.

"Tell her that I'm going to find Prince Piam's cure so she doesn't have to. Oh, and that I borrowed her crystal and I promise to take good care of it."

Trin folded his arms. "No way."

"Please! Otherwise they'll just think I ran away and it'll look even more like I *am* in cahoots with my father!"

"Meylyne, you *can't* go." Train grasped Meylyne's hands with her talons. "The Above-Worldians are total barbarians. If they find out that you're part-garlysle, *and* Meph's daughter, they'll probably roast you on a spit and eat you!" She jutted out her beak. "If you go, I go."

For an instant Meylyne was tempted. Then she shook her head. "No. At least I look like an Above-Worldian. We'll definitely get caught if you come too."

Train opened her beak to argue but Trin cut her off.

"Meylyne is right, and if the Well said so, then she *has* to go."

A voice floated in from the back of the cave.

"Trin, Train—is Meylyne in there with you? I just got a message-mole from her mother. She's looking for her."

The blood drained from Meylyne's face.

"No dad, she's not in here," Trin yelled. "Quick—out through there," he hissed at Meylyne, pointing to an open window above them. He pushed a chair underneath it. "Now, before dad comes in and finds you here!"

Meylyne jumped up.

"Wait!" Train grabbed her wrist. "You can't just go by yourself — it's far too dangerous!"

Meylyne's throat tightened. "Listen, the Well told me to go, so it has to be okay."

Train exchanged a desperate look with Trin.

"She's right. The Well knows what it's doing," he said.

For a second, Train looked as if she would argue. Instead she pressed something into Meylyne's hand. It was a small, pewter locket in the shape of a shield. "Then take this."

Meylyne looked at it. "This is your mother's locket. I can't take it."

"You must," Train insisted. "Mother talks to us through it. She'll tell us if you need our help."

Meylyne's throat tightened. Trin's and Train's mother had died when they were little and her locket was their most beloved possession.

"Hey!" The door handle to Trin's and Train's room rattled and their father's voice boomed from outside. "Why is this door locked? Open up!"

"Sorry Dad," Trin called out. "Didn't mean to do that. I'll open it right now." *Go!* he mouthed to Meylyne.

Meylyne climbed onto the window sill.

"You'll give Mother the message?" she whispered.

Trin and Train nodded. Meylyne gave them a watery smile and then dropped to the ground below. Without a backward glance, she sped away from their cave.

She didn't dare use the entrance to the Above-World that she had used that morning. It was bound to be guarded now.

The only other unguarded entrance that she knew of was by the Wise Well.

Once again, she made her way to the abandoned part of the Between-World. Her fingers played with the pewter locket but she tried not to think of her friends. It was too horrible to imagine never seeing them again. Before she knew it, she was at the Well's edge.

"I'm doing what you said," she called out. "I'm leaving to find Prince Piam's cure."

The Well's waters swirled and bubbled. "I knew you would do the right thing. Farewell, Meylyne."

"Wait!" Panic swelled in Meylyne's chest. "What exactly am I supposed to get from the Valley of Half-Light?"

"Everything you need to know will be told to you, along the way."

"Really?" Meylyne's voice became shrill. "Including how to fend off soul-eating sphers?"

"There is a spell for that, in your Book of Enchantments. Farewell, Meylyne."

"Wait! Please don't go yet. I just need to know—this won't take long, will it? I mean, I'll be home soon, right?"

The Well's waters became still.

"Hello!" Meylyne splashed the water with her hand but the Well remained silent. She was on her own now. Pushing herself to her feet, she trudged over to a cave and threaded her way through the cracked bowls and bottles on the floor to a small staircase in the back. It was dark there and she felt her way along the wall; cobwebs clinging to her hands and face. At the top of the stairs, a dim light outlined a door. She opened it and peeped outside.

A quiet, spacious street met her eyes. This entrance came out in one of Tyr's outlying roads—it had none of the noise and grime of the town square. On either side of her, a row of cedars shielded her from the houses behind them. The entrance was hidden in one of the trees.

Once she was sure no one was around, she crept outside and made her way along the perfectly groomed ice to a field full of cherry-blooms. The crimson flowers looked purple in the dusk and their fragrance perfumed the air. Just beyond them was the stream. It was an uphill walk and she was panting by the time she got there.

Catching her breath, she looked around. The stream was lined by drooping willows and blue ferns. There was no sign of the stalliynx.

Or any living thing, for that matter.

She made her way downstream. About five trees later, she saw something. A spiky fern hid its body but she could see its long gray and white head as it drank from the water.

That must be it!

Meylyne had never met a stalliynx before. They kept to themselves. Licking her lips, she stepped into the moonlight.

"Um, h-hello there," she called out.

The stalliynx lifted its head and looked at her. It was about the size of a horse and had a horse's head but its body was sleek and golden like that of a lion's. Instead of hooves, it had long, sharp talons. Backing away from the stream, it stalked toward her.

Meylyne took a small step away. "I'm Meylyne."

"I know," replied the stalliynx. Its voice reminded her of a bassoon-frog she had once heard singing at night; deep and rich.

"Oh—good." Meylyne produced a nervous smile. "I suppose the Well got a message to you."

The stalliynx nodded. "You ready?"

Meylyne blinked. *No, "hi, nice to meet you, I'm Mr. Stalliynx," or anything like that.*

"I suppose so. Do you know where it is I need to go?"

The stalliynx nodded.

"Oh." Meylyne took stock of its wide and rather high-up back. "It's just . . . I've never actually ridden a stalliynx before. I've never ridden *anything*, for that matter."

The stalliynx lowered itself to the ground.

"Right," Meylyne muttered. Heaving her rucksack over her shoulder, she straddled the stalliynx's back and clutched its thick, white mane as it rose to its feet. She wobbled a bit as it started to walk.

"You understand me? Not used to talking your language," the stallyinx said.

"Yes, thank you."

Meylyne tried to focus on the rhythm of its legs as they walked on, following the stream as it wound through the willows. Once she felt steadier, she looked up at Glendoch's three moons, glowing above her.

"I've never seen the moons before. It was always daytime when I saw the Above-World in Mother's crystal. They're huge!"

"Big and bright," the stalliynx growled. "But don't worry. No one see us. When we reach western plains, we take floating bridge to Valley of Half-Light. No one use bridge now, so no one bother us."

"Why does no one use the bridge any more?"

"No one dare."

Meylyne swallowed. *Of course not,* she thought. *No right-minded Glendochian would leave Glendoch Proper.* The outlands were the home of the exiled ones—witches and other spiteful creatures, like her father.

"So, what's your name?" she asked, wanting to change the subject.

"Hopexivaffoplos-ploossenaagen. Mister."

"Hopeggsy—what?"

"You call me Hope."

Meylyne breathed a sigh of relief. "Hope it is."

By now they had reached the edge of a forest. An eerie silence enveloped them as they entered it. Meylyne's head swiveled from side to side as she took in the old, white trees looming up before them, shafts of moonlight filtering through the branchless trunks.

"This place is spooky," she whispered.

Hope did not reply. Meylyne shifted uncomfortably as a pang of guilt stabbed her.

"I am sorry that you have to do all this because of me," she said.

"Request come from Well. No need apologize. Well very wise."

"Yes—usually I think so too, but right now this whole thing seems like the *opposite* of wise. How long will it take us to get to the Valley?"

"Week."

Meylyne's shoulders sagged. "So I have one week to learn the spell to keep the sphers away."

"That hard?"

"Most likely! And then I don't even know what I'm supposed to find once I'm there. Why would the prince's cure be *there* of all places?"

Hope was silent for a minute. "What Well say?"

"Just that I would learn whatever I needed along the way. Oh . . . and to practice my sorcery. As if *that* will do any good."

A dark shadow scuttled up one of the trees. Meylyne turned to see a rat-like creature with a scorpion's tail, glaring at her as she rode by.

"Aah!" she shrieked. "What is that?"

Hope shied away, his head snapping back to see. "Merdrat."

"A *merdrat?*" Meylyne's entire body shuddered. "Ugh! Here I am, worrying about what to do once I get to the Valley, when really it'll be a miracle if we make it there at all."

Hope chuckled. "Don't worry. I get you to Valley. That *easy* part."

5

An Unfortunate Oversight

A FEW HOURS LATER, MEYLYNE AND HOPE STOOD AT the entrance of a narrow, wooden bridge. Part-suspension, part-floating, it zig-zagged over Glendoch's western plains before disappearing into the mountains. Meylyne stared at its splintered planks and wonky railing.

"Um, is this old bridge the *only* way to the Valley of Half-Light?"

"It is."

Meylyne shivered, drawing her hood tightly around her head. It was weird having nothing but the sky above her. Up ahead, the ground dropped away fifty feet and the ice below was ripped into ragged, razor-sharp peaks.

"And you're sure it's safe to cross?"

Hope walked onto the bridge. "Safe enough."

"Whoa!" Meylyne gripped even more tightly to Hope's mane. "Really? It's just it sort of looks like the *opposite* of safe."

A wind blew up, muffling Meylyne's words and causing her eyes to smart from the ice-chips whirling around. Looking down, she felt her stomach tighten. A yawning chasm, like a monster's mouth with icy teeth, appeared below her.

She clamped herself around Hope, shouting, "Maybe this isn't such a good idea after all. Let's just turn around."

Hope stalked on as if he hadn't heard her.

"Hope—" Meylyne's words were drowned out as the wind howled even louder, pelting her with ice. It felt like someone was throwing pins in her face and she buried her head in Hope's mane. This felt a tiny bit better until a huge gust of wind slammed into them. Hope stumbled from the force of it.

For a second she debated sliding off his back and making a run for it but then another gust of wind slammed into her. She clung even more tightly to him. The only thing worse than being stuck on this bridge with Hope would be being stuck there without him.

From underneath her fur-trimmed cloak, she could feel his muscles moving up and down as he plodded forward. After a while she loosened her vice-like grip on him. Despite the storm raging around them, he seemed to know what he was doing. Eventually, the wind died down. Lifting up her hood, Meylyne saw that the bridge was wider now and not quite so rickety.

"Wow. I can't believe you got us through that bit. This doesn't look nearly as bad . . ."

A noise sounded in the distance and she stopped mid-sentence.

"Did you hear that?" she asked.

The noise came again, a mournful wailing sound. Her scalp prickled. "Hope, what is that?"

"Hyldas coming."

"Hyldas?" Meylyne's voice became hoarse. "No way."

Craning back her neck, she searched the sky. A speck

appeared in front of one of the moons. Growing larger and larger, it soon became a black cloud blotting out the moon entirely. Panic coursed through Meylyne's veins and she tugged desperately on Hope's mane.

"What are we going to do, Hope? There's nowhere to hide!"

"Nothing. Hyldas not interested in us."

Meylyne did not believe him, especially as she felt him tense beneath her. She looked up again. As the cloud got closer, it started to break up. Now she could see at least fifty winged women and girls with long black hair, flowing behind them. A few seconds later, they were directly above Meylyne and Hope. Meylyne could not make out their faces but she had heard they were beautiful, with blue-black skin and eyes like aquamarine. Their enormous wings pulsed together as if they were attached to each other.

Meylyne held her breath, convinced they would swoop down and scoop her up at any minute. Her eyes remained riveted on them as they passed by, their forms melting into one again.

A minute later, they were gone.

Meylyne exhaled slowly.

"I can't *believe* a pack of Hyldas just flew over us!"

She had only read about Hyldas before. Guardians of the warrior-realm, it was their job to carry off the spirits of those killed in war. Supposedly they were fearsome creatures with little regard for the living. It did not do to cross paths with them.

"They must be off to a battle, right?"

Hope nodded. "Take away spirits of battle-slain."

Meylyne suddenly remembered what Queen Emery had said about war being near.

"They weren't flying toward Glendoch Proper, were they?"

"No. Toward Celadonia. Our neighbor to west."

"Phew. You know Hyldas are supposed to be *super*-scary. They can turn you to stone just by looking at you!"

"Not true," Hope replied.

Meylyne ignored him. She felt exhilarated with their escape. "I can't wait to tell Trin and Train about this . . ."

Hope remained silent while she babbled on. Then, as the excitement drained from her body, her mind became leaden. Sitting up took far too much effort, and she lay down on Hope's neck, weaving her hands and arms through the knots in his mane so she didn't have to hold on. He was warm, his steady gait soothing. She'd just close her eyes for a little bit. No way would she fall asleep.

She woke up bathed in the pink blush of dawn. At first, her mind struggled to understand why she was outside, lying on the most uncomfortable bed ever, with her arms stretched forward, wrapped in rope. Then all the events from the past day and night flooded her mind. Gingerly, she unraveled her arms from Hope's mane, every movement sending daggers of pain through her shoulders.

"Everything hurts!" she moaned as she tried to sit up. Her back felt like someone was wringing her out like a wet cloth. Despite that, when she finally made it to sitting upright, she could not help but be awed by the ice-clad mountains surrounding them. They were in a small clearing, with hot springs bubbling to their right. Steam rose off them, warming the air around Meylyne and Hope.

"Nice sleep?" Hope asked.

"I guess so," she grumbled. She wiggled her feet to try to bring back some feeling into her legs, which were so stiff she was convinced she would be permanently bow-legged. Then she realized that Hope had been probably walking all night and immediately felt bad. He was sure to feel worse than she did.

"Do you want to sleep now?"

Hope shook his head. "Not tired. Eat breakfast."

Meylyne reached into her rucksack and pulled out the bag of daffy seeds. Dumping some into her hand, she fed Hope before cramming the rest in her mouth. It was probably the world's worst breakfast. A tingle between her shoulder blades made her shiver and she reached back into her rucksack.

Hope would get a shock if I forgot to take these, she thought as she took out a bottle of purple pills. She washed one down with a swig from her water-pouch and then tried to squeeze some water into Hope's mouth. A lot of it spilled on the ground, which was covered with a green, spongy-looking plant she had never seen before.

"What's all this stuff covering the bridge?" she asked.

"Moss. Ready?"

"Hang on." Meylyne stuffed the pouch back into her bag. Something in Hope's voice made her uneasy. "Ready for what?"

"Running!"

Meylyne's stomach gave a terrible lurch as Hope sprang forward. She was suddenly very much awake. Clutching his mane, she gripped his body with her thighs as everything around her became a blur.

"Aaaahhhhhhhhh," she shrieked. "Slow down already!"

Hope whinnied gleefully in his own language and went even faster.

Meylyne tilted backward as Hope charged up the mountain, her arms shaking with the effort of holding on. For a while, everything blurred by in streaks of white, green and blue. Then, up ahead, she saw the bridge curve around and leave the mountainside altogether.

"Whoooooooaaaaaaaaaaahhhhh!" she shrieked. "Slow *down!*"

Before she knew it, the bridge rose off the mountain, floating free-form in the air. Now there was nothing on either side of her but blue sky and the flaming yellow-orange orb of the sun. Her legs tightened around Hope while her hair streamed in the wind. Just as her muscles began to throb from holding on, Hope slowed to a canter. They had reached the next mountain in the range.

"This is more like it!" Meylyne shouted. "Don't go any faster!"

To her relief, Hope settled into this slower pace. They continued on like this for hours, intermittently slowing to a trot until the sun was directly above them. Vast lemon trees grew on either side, their boughs hanging low with fruit.

Finally, Hope slowed to a standstill.

"Lunch-time," he panted.

Meylyne whimpered as her fingers straightened out, one by one. They had cramped into claws around Hope's mane. Gritting her teeth, she maneuvered one of her legs over his back and slid off, crying out as she landed on the ground like a sack of potatoes.

"You did well," Hope said. "Natural rider."

Meylyne glared at him. The aches she had felt in the morning were nothing compared to the agony she was in now. She felt like little pokers were stabbing into muscles she didn't even know she had.

"I don't care how well I did. I was really scared when you were galloping like that. Now I can't move!"

Plucking off a lemon, Hope chomped on it without displaying a shred of remorse. Meylyne fiddled with the buckle on her rucksack, her fingers barely functioning. The buckle finally slid open and she pulled out some figs. Her water-pouch rolled out with them.

"Open, please." Hope nudged the pouch with his nose.

Meylyne unscrewed the top and thrust the pouch at him. She was determined not to talk to him until he apologized.

Two dragon-flies buzzed by, their iridescent blue-green wings shimmering in the sun. Meylyne munched on some figs and for a while the two sat in silence. As the sun warmed her face, the tension oozed out of her muscles and her bad mood started to lift. She reached for her pouch but when she put it to her lips, only a drop came out. Her temper flared up again.

"Hope! You drank all the water!"

Hope blinked. "That all you brought?"

"Of course it is!" The figs had made her very thirsty. "Now what am I supposed to drink?"

"That *really* all you brought?"

"Yes, it's really all I brought. I guess we'll have to fill it up when it rains."

"What if no rain? No water on bridge!"

Meylyne shrugged and immediately wished she hadn't as

the feeling of hot pokers jabbed into her back again. "Why wouldn't it rain here? It always rains in Glendoch Proper."

"Not here."

Meylyne's bad mood worsened.

So what—now it's my fault that we're out of water? Like I was supposed to know it doesn't rain on this stupid bridge.

Once again, silence descended upon the two of them. After a while, Meylyne's eyelids drooped shut and she was almost asleep when Hope nudged her.

"You conjure water," he said.

Meylyne opened one baleful eye.

"What?"

"We need water. You sorceress. Conjure it!"

Meylyne snorted and shut her eye again.

Hope nudged her again. "Come on!"

With a huge groan, Meylyne sat up. "Look. I am *terrible* at alchemy, okay? I couldn't possibly conjure up water—it's a two-part transformation; a level Five spell. I'm only up to level Two." She scowled. "It's where I've been stuck my whole life. I've had so many accidents, Mother has forbidden me to practice in our cave!"

Hope studied her for a minute.

"You practice with me. I no mind accidents." He looked up at the sky. "Now we get going—time for practice later. No excuses!"

By now, the sun had dipped down half-way into the sky. Meylyne climbed up on Hope's back. Now she felt achy *and* discouraged. Dwelling on her alchemical incompetence always put her in a bad mood, and her dry, scratchy throat wasn't helping matters.

As Hope broke into a canter, she braced herself for him to start galloping again. Much to her relief, he stayed at the slower pace. The lemon trees thinned out in a blur of green and yellow, replaced by a line of fragrant mimosa-trees. Long, purple sticks and white, feathery silkweed poked up between them. The sun hung low in the sky when he stopped.

"Off, please," he said, his voice low and urgent.

Meylyne's body shook with fatigue as he sank to the ground and she slid off him. There was a faint scent of lavender in the air, which she might have enjoyed were she not so exhausted. She had a dull headache and her mouth felt horribly dry and sticky. Looking at Hope, she noticed that his lips and back were flecked with foam. This lack of water was a bigger deal than she'd thought.

"We really have to find some water, don't we Hope?"

"Ssshh." Hope began sniffing around one of the trees. "Look."

On the ground before him was a large, greenish-black feather; as long as Meylyne's arm.

"Belongs to Hylda," Hope said. "Come."

Hope stalked through the silkweed, stopping at the gnarled trunk of a mimosa-tree. Meylyne followed him. They were right at the edge of the bridge.

"As thought," he said. "Bats build nests underneath this bridge. Look."

Dropping to all fours, Meylyne lowered herself to the ground and cautiously peered down below. She could just about see some brown, ropy material hanging beneath her.

"How weird. Bats built this? It's huge—looks more like a cave than a nest. How'd you know it was here?"

"Hylda feather. Hyldas use caves to sleep in at night."

An icy finger snaked its way up Meylyne's spine and she backed away from the edge of the bridge.

"Well let's get out of here then! We can't stay here with a pack of Hyldas right beneath us!"

Hope fixed her in his gaze. "Hyldas have water."

All the hairs rose on Meylyne's body. "And what—you're going to steal it from them?"

"No. You are."

6

The Thief

"WHAT?" MEYLYNE SCREECHED. "NO *WAY!*"

"I can't climb down into cave. You can," Hope said. "Hyldas sleep very deep. Carry with them reed bags filled with water. You get one—last us till Valley of Half-Light."

"Oh right. And get turned to stone if a Hylda wakes up? I don't think so!"

"That not happen." Hope's tone turned desperate. "Listen—I need water *bad*. You too, soon. We have no choice!"

"No choice?" Now it was Meylyne's turn to sound desperate. "I think just keeping going is a perfectly good choice! I'm sure it will rain or something."

Hope sniffed the air. "It no rain for two weeks. We no last two *days*."

Meylyne stared at Hope. His eyes were dull and his mouth was still flecked with foam. They really had to find water fast. But stealing from a pack of Hyldas—

She sunk her head in her hands.

"I can't, Hope. I just can't!"

"I no ask if too dangerous," Hope insisted. "As soon as night fall, Hyldas sleep. They sleep like dead."

The air was already plum-colored with dusk. It would be nightfall soon.

"But how will I see anything down there?"

"Hyldas wear stones around their necks. Aquamins. Sacred stones help them talk to dead. They glow in dark."

Meylyne wrung her hands. Hope was not going to let this drop.

"Is there *nowhere* else we can get water?"

"No. Almost at drylands."

Meylyne had heard that the drylands were beautiful, like blankets of golden sand. And completely devoid of water. She was out of arguments.

"You're sure—you're *absolutely* sure—there's no way the Hyldas will wake up?"

Hope nodded.

"All right, I'll do it."

Hope sank to the ground.

"Thank you. Now we wait for dark to come."

Meylyne sat down next to him. Somewhere in the distance, an owl hooted. Behind her the purple sticks melted into the indigo light and the mimosa-trees rustled faintly. Night was falling fast. Drumming her fingers on the ground, she tried not to think. This was worse than waiting for her mother to come home when one of her messed-up spells had flooded their kitchen with caramel. Finally Hope nudged her.

"Time."

Meylyne's heart began to hammer.

"I wait here for you," Hope said reassuringly. "This all be finished in no time."

"Right."

Meylyne crawled toward the edge of the bridge and peered over. In the moonlight, she saw that the fibrous wall of the nest had been woven into criss-crosses and fastened onto purple sticks, poking through cracks in the bridge.

She grasped two of the sticks. They seemed sturdy enough. Reaching down a leg, she searched with her foot for something resembling a rung in the nest's fibers. *There!* She reached down another foot and cautiously lowered herself into the nest.

At first, she couldn't see anything but dots of pale blue light.

Those must be the aquamins.

As her eyes adjusted to the darkness, she saw that the cave floor was covered with big, black mounds.

Hyldas!

She broke into a cold sweat. Forcing herself to crawl forward, she reached the first mound. The Hylda was lying on her back; the pale blue stone on her chest radiating a small halo of light. Just beneath the blue glow was a strap of some sort. Moving closer, Meylyne saw that it was attached to a bag.

That must be it!

Willing her hand to stop shaking, Meylyne took hold of the bag, but when she pulled it toward her, it tugged against something. Mercifully, the Hylda did not stir.

What's it caught on?

Her eyes followed the strap up, and into the Hylda's long black hair.

You have to be joking. She's wearing the bag around her neck!

Meylyne closed her eyes. Part of her wanted nothing more than to give up and get out of there as fast as possible. *But you've come this far,* another part of her insisted. *You can't leave without the bag now!*

With a deep breath, she grasped the strap in one hand while reaching her other hand underneath the Hylda's head. A few strands of hair fell from the Hylda's face, but she didn't wake up. Meylyne slowly lifted up the Hylda's head and pulled the strap out and over the top of it.

The Hylda still did not stir. She lay as motionless as a statue.

And the strap was free!

Meylyne felt giddy with amazement. She had actually done it! Turning around, she hung the bag around her neck and crawled toward the front of the cave as fast as she could. She was almost at the cave entrance when a voice chirped from above—

"Take me with you."

Meylyne gave a small shriek and clamped a hand over her mouth, her head snapping up to see where the voice came from. Hanging on the wall was a cage and in it, a small blue bird.

"Please." Its voice was louder now. "You can't leave me here."

Something stirred in the cave. Panic welled inside Meylyne.

"Sshhh! You'll wake up the Hyldas!"

"Then hurry up and get me out of here!"

The bird's voice was even louder now. Desperate to shut it up, Meylyne sprang to her feet.

"All right! Just be quiet! *Please!*"

She grabbed the cage but as she tried to unhook it, she dislodged something soft and fluttery. It landed on the cave floor and, to her utter horror, gave an ear-shattering scream.

Oh no—it's a bat!

Everything that happened next was a blur. Hearing noises from within the cave, she ran blindly for the cave entrance. Behind her the bird pleaded with her to come back as she clambered up the ropy wall. Hope waited for her at the top. Grabbing the back of her cape in his talons, he hoisted her up.

"Bird . . . bat . . ." Meylyne panted, trying to explain. She trailed off as a black, flapping cloud emerged over the side of the bridge.

"Hyldas!"

She and Hope shrank into one another as the Hyldas swarmed around them. They were every bit as magnificent as Meylyne had heard—tall and muscular, with gleaming blue-black skin and piercing blue eyes. They wore greenish-black feather-dresses. Or maybe the feathers were part of them. It was impossible to tell. Within seconds, they had surrounded Meylyne and Hope.

One of them stepped forward. She wore a garland of leaves and berries around her head.

"So. You dare steal from us."

Her voice was low and musical, and her pale blue eyes glowed with fire.

"Only wanted some water," Hope said loudly. "Didn't think you miss it."

"Only water?" The Hylda gave Meylyne a cool look. "I don't think so."

Meylyne pressed herself into Hope's side.

"It's true," she whispered, her voice barely audible. "Please don't turn me into stone."

"You tried to steal the bird!"

"The bird? No! It *begged* me to take it with me! I . . . I was afraid you'd all wake up if I didn't do as it said. I promise!"

The Hylda reached out a hand to Meylyne until it was inches from her nose. There were feathers attached to her wrists and her fingernails were curved, like claws.

"First you steal, and now you lie."

"Meylyne no liar," Hope growled.

The Hylda turned on Hope.

"Impossible! The bird speaks the tongue of the dead—only the aquamins can understand it."

She turned back to Meylyne. "You came here to finish off what you started, didn't you?"

Meylyne could only stare at her, bewildered. She opened her mouth but no words came out. She shook her head.

"Fetch the bird!" the leader roared.

There was a ripple in the crowd. Seconds later, another Hylda appeared, holding the birdcage. The bird cocked its head at Meylyne, and mumbled something.

"All right," the leader sneered at Meylyne. "You who understands the dead—what did the bird just say?"

Meylyne stared desperately at the bird.

"I don't know—it spoke too softly!"

"Just as I thought," the leader hissed, her eyes blazing. "Nothing but lies!"

Meylyne raised her hands before her face, sure she would turn into stone at any second. Then she heard the bird chirp,

"I said I was sorry—I didn't mean to get you in trouble."

"It said it was sorry it didn't mean to get me in trouble!" Meylyne blurted.

Silence. Then another voice—singsong and not quite there—

It is true.

The leader held her aquamin up in front of her face. "Are you sure?" she asked it.

Yes. She's a Hearer.

The words reverberated inside Meylyne's head. They came from the aquamin.

"What's going on?" she whispered to Hope.

"Aquamin speaking to Hylda," Hope replied. "They sacred—speak to dead. Translate for Hyldas when carry off battle-slain."

The Hylda looked down at Meylyne.

"Well, well, well. A human Hearer."

She turned to Hope. "I knew your kind could still Hear. But I thought yours," she turned her gaze back to Meylyne, "never learned the skills of your elders."

"No, the humans never learned the language of nature, but I'm part-garlysle," Meylyne stammered.

Now there was murmuring among the Hyldas and the leader's eyes showed a hint of curiosity.

"It is a well-known fact that most garlysles lost their Hearing skills years ago. There is but one garlysle that we know of that can still Hear—your notorious outlaw, Meph."

Her lips twitched in a smirk.

"You are *clearly* not he."

Meylyne bristled at the snickers this remark provoked. If there was one thing Meph had going for him, it was that he was a force to be reckoned with. Not so much herself.

"No, but I am his daughter," she retorted.

There was dead silence. Another murmur rippled among the Hyldas as their eyes fastened upon her.

Now she'd done it. Meylyne wished she could bite back the words.

Another Hylda came forward. Her hair was streaked with white and her face was as mottled as a rotten crab-apple. She circled Meylyne.

"If *that* is true, then you are also the daughter of Glendoch's sorceress, Ellenyr."

Meylyne felt the hairs prickle on the back of her neck. "How do you know that?"

"There is unrest in Glendoch. Unrest precedes war. Most likely, we will be needed there soon enough." The old Hylda shrugged. "We make it our business to understand the people with whom we shall soon become acquainted."

She drew nearer to Meylyne.

"So, it is true then—you are the sorceress's daughter. Do you, too, have alchemical powers?"

"Sort of," Meylyne mumbled.

"Sort of," the old Hylda echoed, glancing at the leader.

The leader regarded Meylyne. After a moment's pause, she took the cage from the Hylda next to her and thrust it at Meylyne.

"Well, sort-of-sorceress, I believe there is a way for us to wipe the slate clean. You see, this is no ordinary bird. Once it was a mighty warrior but then an assassin struck him down. The warrior's essence escaped the attack, but his assassin captured it and trapped it in the body of this bird. The assassin left it with the sphers to finish it off."

Meylyne shuddered.

"Yes, we all know how *that* would have ended. Luckily for the warrior, our aquamins instructed us to retrieve him before that could happen. Now he must be returned to his original state if he is to fulfill his life's purpose."

The leader paused, as if waiting for a response.

"Um. Okay," Meylyne said with a shrug.

"And for that, we need a sorceress."

Meylyne was confused as the leader smiled, revealing silver, pointed teeth. Then comprehension dawned on her and her look of puzzlement turned to one of disbelief.

"You're joking, right? You don't honestly believe *I* can do that!"

"Oh but you must, if you and your friend wish to go free."

Meylyne heard herself laugh hysterically.

"Look, I'm really, *really* bad at sorcery. I couldn't possibly get a spell like that right!"

The leader bent down until her eyes were inches from Meylyne's.

"I'm not interested in excuses, sorceress. You must free him, unless you want to end up in the Cave of Nhyrr."

Meylyne cringed. The Cave of Nhyrr was where the battle-slain with impure hearts were taken to sleep forever. Once inside, there was no waking up.

"Please," she begged. "Please don't ask —"

Suddenly, all the Hyldas' aquamins blazed with electric-blue light.

"Time to depart," the leader shouted. "The battle of Wahir-Pet is about to begin!" She faced Meylyne. "Time runs short, sorceress. What is it to be?"

Hope thrust Meylyne's bag at her. "Just do spell best you can," he urged.

"Is no one listening to me?" Meylyne yanked out her book. The pages trembled as she flipped through them. "See!" She jammed her finger into the middle of the book, her eyes pleading with the leader. "Restoring stolen essences is a Level Seven incantation. I'm only at Level Two!"

Two Hyldas grabbed Hope's mane, unfurling their wings.

"Meylyne do spell," Hope cried. "Now!"

"*Okay!* Just give me a second!"

Tears welled up in Meylyne's eyes as she skimmed through the incantation. She could just about pronounce all the words it required. *But what's that bit in the middle about? It doesn't make any sense.* She glanced at the bird, feeling like an executioner descending upon her victim.

"Hurry!" the leader spat.

Meylyne stuck out her hand. "Fine. I need the bird to sit here."

The leader unhooked the cage and the bird flew into Meylyne's hand. Taking a deep breath, she began to gurgle, then gagged like she had a bone stuck in her throat. The bird closed its eyes and rolled onto its back.

Meylyne licked her lips. *Just keep going.*

Moving to the third part of the spell, she chanted in an ancient Glendochian dialect. Toward the end of the chant, she moved her hand over the bird's body and closed her eyes.

". . . eco yabboe," she finished. Opening her eyes, she placed the bird on the ground and waited.

Nothing happened.

Meylyne stared at the bird, willing it to change into a

warrior, or at the very least to open its eyes and not be dead. One minute stretched into two.

"What have you done to him?" the leader growled at Meylyne.

"I don't—"

"Look!" Hope barked.

Meylyne's head snapped back to face the bird and her mouth fell open.

The bird's spindly legs were lengthening while its claws plumped up into boots. Its wings grew and shrank at the same time into thin, feathered arms. Its head and chest were expanding like a balloon being blown up. There was a loud RRRIP and all the feathers flew off his body.

"Aaaah!" Meylyne shrieked. "Ewww!" She spat out a mouthful of feathers, then waved her arms in front of her face to clear the air around her.

No way!

There, on the ground where the bird had been, sat a boy. He wore a greenish-brown jacket with trousers to match. The trousers were tucked into clunky gray boots. Meylyne had never seen clothes like his before. Nor had she seen anyone his size.

What is he, like, a foot tall?

"Well done, sorceress," said the leader. "You did it."

7

Blue

MEYLYNE LOOKED AT THE BOY ON THE GROUND AND almost laughed aloud.

Well done? He's a foot tall!

"Here." The leader dropped a reed bag at her feet. "Try not to steal anything else, sorceress. It would be good for you to make it home unharmed. Something tells me you'll be needed there soon enough." She nodded toward the boy. "And take him with you. You will want a good warrior on your side."

Before Meylyne could ask her what she meant, the leader unfurled her enormous wings and shot off into the air. All the other Hyldas followed, spiraling past the moons like a plume of smoke. In seconds they were gone.

Meylyne stared at Hope. It was so quiet now that she could hear leaves rustling in the tree-tops. Hard to believe they had just been seconds away from permanent sleep or petrification or who-knows-what those terrifying creatures chose to do to them. Her legs turned to jelly and she sank to the ground.

"You did *great*, Meylyne."

Hope's eyes shone with admiration as he nosed the reed bag toward her. "Open please."

Feeling like one in a dream, Meylyne poured some water into Hope's mouth. He gulped it down with gusto, and then pushed the bag toward Meylyne.

"Now you."

Meylyne took a long drink. She had forgotten how thirsty she was. The water cleared her mind and she felt a little less shaky.

"Now give some to him," Hope said.

Meylyne looked at the boy, still sitting on the ground. The boy that, a few minutes ago, was a bird. He appeared as dazed as she felt. She held out the reed bag to him, and he reached out his hand but instead of taking the bag, he wiggled his fingers and began touching his cheeks and nose. Meylyne jumped as he bounded to his feet, crying, "Look at me! I'm a *person* again! Two arms, two legs, no feathers . . ."

He stared at Meylyne.

"But what's up with my size? Did you mean to make me so short?"

He and Meylyne were eye-level, despite the fact that she was sitting down. At least he wasn't *quite* as short as she had thought. She shook her head.

"Oh." For a second his face fell but it brightened up almost immediately. "Well never mind—you can always get that right later." Patting his jacket, he chuckled. "At least I've got clothes on, right? This must be what I was wearing when I was attacked. And look!"

Meylyne flinched as he pulled out a dagger from his belt.

"I really *am* a warrior—just like those Hylda-ladies said!"

Meylyne was having a hard time keeping up with him.

"Well, of course. Why wouldn't you be?"

"Because I don't remember anything. Not where I'm from. Not my name. Nothing. If the Hyldas say I'm a warrior, then I guess I am but I don't *remember* it."

"You don't remember *anything*? What about who attacked you?"

A haunted look crossed the boy's face.

"Nope. If the Hyldas hadn't explained it to me, I still wouldn't know what had happened. I just woke up one day in the body of a bird! I knew that was *wrong*, you know—I knew I was meant to be human, but that's about it."

"How awful!" Meylyne exclaimed.

"Oh *that* wasn't the awful bit. What was awful was the sickness. All those ghostly things floating around me. The sadness. I could never sleep. I just got weaker and weaker."

Meylyne shivered. "Well yeah—the sphers were eating your essence. Thank goodness the Hyldas saved you."

The boy nodded. "Tell me about it! Can't say I was too thrilled to be with those scary bird-ladies, but they were a heck of a lot better than the sphers." He grinned at Meylyne. "And then *you* came along. How lucky am I?"

Meylyne raised her eyebrows. To say he was "lucky" seemed like a stretch.

So, you don't even remember your name?"

"Naah. The Hyldas called me Blue but I'm pretty sure that was just a nickname they gave me."

"We call you Blue then. I Hope, and that Meylyne," Hope said.

"Great to meet you both!"

Blue grinned and stuck out his hand to Meylyne. Smiling warily, she gave it a shake.

"So, er, what is this place?" Blue asked, gesturing around him.

"This is Glendoch. Glendoch's Outlands, to be precise," Meylyne explained. "Hope and I are from Glendoch Proper."

She debated telling him about the Above-World and the Between-World, but decided it was too much information at once.

"You're definitely not from around here," she added. "I've never heard anyone talk like you before."

"Yeah. Pretty sure that where *I'm* from people aren't magical. And animals don't talk."

"Well, there aren't that many alchemists left in Glendoch either," Meylyne replied. "Aside from my mother and me, I don't know any others."

"Mmm." Blue studied Meylyne for a moment. "So, is there a spell to get me back to my normal height?"

"How you know that *not* your normal height?" Hope interjected. "You remember nothing."

Blue frowned while he thought about this.

"Good point. I *don't* know. Man, I need my memory back!"

He turned back to Meylyne. "Is there a spell for that too?"

Pulling out her quilt, Meylyne wrapped it around her shoulders. She suddenly felt exhausted.

"Mmm-hmm."

"Well can you do it now?"

"*I* can't do it at all. You'd need a decent sorceress for that, like my mother."

"No," Hope cut in. "You *are* decent sorceress. You get Blue *almost* back to normal!"

Meylyne sighed. There was no way to explain how she'd only got Blue's size wrong with such a complicated incantation when she had failed in so many simpler ones before. It must have been luck. She pulled out some seeds from her bag and shrugged.

Blue stared at Meylyne, obviously waiting for her to reply. When she remained silent, he said, "Fine. We'll just ask your mom to fix me."

Meylyne choked on the seeds she had put in her mouth. She could just imagine the look on her mother's face if she showed up with Blue.

"That's not a good idea."

"Why not? The Hylda said you should take me with you!"

Meylyne sunk her head in her hands and groaned. This was the last thing she needed. She wasn't even sure she could get herself home, let alone some pint-sized boy-warrior from who-knew-where.

"I know what the Hylda said, but here's the thing, Blue. Before I can go home, I have to find something in the Valley of Half-Light. I *highly* doubt you want to go back there!"

All the color drained from Blue's face.

"You're joking right?" He gave a violent shudder. "You'd *better* be a decent sorceress if you plan to go there."

Meylyne's shoulders sagged.

"Yes, well, that's the problem. Trust me, you're better off *not* coming with us."

"If Hylda say to bring him then we should," Hope countered. "She say battle brewing in Glendoch. Need warrior!"

Meylyne was about to argue when she remembered what Queen Emery had said about war being near. At the time she had thought the queen said it to justify sending her mother to the Valley of Half-Light. But maybe she was telling the truth.

"Well?" Blue prompted.

Scrunching up her bag as a pillow, Meylyne lay down on the ground and held up the edge of her quilt to Blue.

"I'm too tired to think right now. Let's just go to sleep and we'll work it all out in the morning."

"Go to sleep?" Blue sounded incredulous.

Hope lowered himself to the ground. "Meylyne right. We sleep now. Think clearer in morning."

After a moment, Blue lay down too, but his eyes remained open and alert. He drew out his dagger and rested it on his chest, its tip gleaming in a splash of moonlight.

You know, it wouldn't be so bad to have him with us, Meylyne thought groggily. *The Hylda's right. A warrior might come in handy. Pint-sized or not …*

Her thoughts jumbled together as she slid into sleep. When she woke up, a few hours later, the night had brightened into dawn. Pushing herself up, she cried out as her back erupted in pain.

There was a flash to her right. Blue was on his feet, dagger in hand. Hope also leapt up and everything from the night—the Hyldas, Blue—flooded into her mind.

"Sorry! It's just me," she said, wincing. "I hurt all over!"

Blue put away his dagger. A fine mist hovered above the ground and the trees were outlined in gold. The undergrowth rustled as a tiny vole-fox poked out its head, then pulled it back in. Everything was quiet until Blue's stomach emitted a loud growl.

Meylyne pushed her bag toward him. "We have seeds or figs. Not much of a breakfast but help yourself."

Blue popped a fig in his mouth.

"Here's what I'm thinking," he said, his cheek bulging. "How about if I come with you *almost* to the Valley of Half-Light. I'll wait for you while you find whatever it is you're looking for and then we'll all go home—to *your* home, that is, where your mom can fix me. Whaddya think?"

Meylyne scratched her arm. A rock had dug into it all night and now it itched.

"I suppose it's not a terrible idea. What do you think Hope?"

Hope was quiet for a minute.

"You remember *nothing* about what happen to you? Not who attack you or why?"

Blue shook his head. "Not a thing."

"Must be significant, if Aquamins tell Hyldas to rescue you," Hope said. "Agree with Meylyne—you come with us, but we need watch out. They probably try attack you again!"

Blue's eyes widened.

"I hadn't thought of that. If I come with you, I could put you guys in danger."

"No—you mighty warrior. You *protect* us from danger."

Meylyne arched an eyebrow. She was more inclined to agree with Blue. Things were bad enough without throwing this into the mix.

Blue jammed his hands into his pockets. "I can't believe this. I'm finally human again . . . but because of that, I'm a target!" His eyes darted between Meylyne and Hope. "And so are you!"

A chill ran through Meylyne.

"Well, look on the bright side. There is no way your assassin would *ever* expect you to go *back* to the Valley of Half-Light."

Blue chuckled mirthlessly.

"No arguing that. Why are *you* going there?"

"That's kind of a long story." With a groan, Meylyne stood up. Between all the riding and climbing, every single one of her muscles felt like it had been teased apart and pounded with a hammer. "I'll tell you later. Right now, as much as I hate to, we should get going. You ready?"

Blue jumped to his feet but Hope stayed where he was. Meylyne looked at him impatiently.

"Come on then!"

"Not yet. You need practice alchemy."

"What, *now?* We're sort of in a hurry here!"

"Yes, and almost at Valley! Need learn incantation to protect us from sphers!"

Meylyne opened her mouth to protest, and then shut it again. It was clear he wasn't budging. The fact that he was right didn't help matters. She yanked her spell book out of her bag, muttering,

"This is just great. I'm in pain. I'm being hunted. And now I have to do the one thing I hate most. Fine! I'll practice for half an hour. And then we're off!"

8

An Unwanted Guest

SUNLIGHT STREAMED THROUGH THE BRANCHES OF THE mimosa trees, none of which penetrated Meylyne's dark mood. Spell practice had not gone well.

As usual, she fumed inwardly.

It had been a few hours since they had set off and the bridge slowly tilted toward the ground. The trees thinned out, revealing an expanse of sand that seemed to stretch for miles on either side. It swirled in mysterious patterns around the green, spiky plants that sprung up, here and there. Every now and then, gusts of wind whipped up the sand. Meylyne shut her eyes but could not do anything about the grains getting into her clothes. Soon everything felt scratchy against her skin.

By the time they stopped for lunch, the sun was a searing blast that made the air wobble and pools shimmer on the ground ahead of them. Meylyne's skin stung with every step, rubbed raw from her sandpaper-like clothes. She and Blue set about gathering up some of the spiky plants to make a tent with her quilt. Sweat pooled on her brow as she crawled underneath it. Even with the shade, the heat was maddening. She chugged down some luke-warm water, and then rummaged around in her bag for some food.

"This is all we have for lunch," she grumbled, pulling out a stale loaf of bread and some figs.

Squeezing himself between Hope and Meylyne, Blue broke off a piece of bread and scraped some mold off it.

"If you don't mind my saying so, you don't exactly seem prepared for this journey of yours," he said.

Meylyne wriggled back, the sensation of someone touching her skin unbearable.

"It's not as if I had *time* to prepare. I didn't get myself into this mess on purpose you know!"

"What mess?"

Meylyne bit savagely into a fig. "I'll tell you later."

Blue took a glug of water. "Lemme guess—this is a punishment for some spell you really messed up. Kinda like setting those bushes on fire this morning."

Meylyne turned her back on him.

"Oh come on!" Blue chortled. "Can't you take a joke?"

"No! And I'm not in the mood to rehash why I'm here. It's embarrassing!"

"Er, maybe you hadn't noticed but I'm a foot tall. Don't talk to *me* about embarrassing!"

The edges of Meylyne's dark mood lifted a little and she giggled, despite her aggravation. She turned back to face Blue.

"*Please* tell me why you're here," he begged.

Meylyne hesitated a moment longer before relenting.

"Fine. I'll tell you the short version and do *not* interrupt me!"

Blue pretended to zip his mouth shut, and then listened attentively as Meylyne explained everything from her mother losing her opal, to her falling on the prince, to Queen Emery ordering her mother to cure him.

". . . it was either do as the Well said, or end up in the Shadow Cellars and possibly the Beneath-World," she finished. "So here I am. Make sense?"

"Yeah, not really." Blue stared at her. "I mean, was it worth it? Breaking a . . . watchamacallit—Golden Rule and all that—for some *stone?*"

"*First* Rule. And no, it wasn't worth it. It was the stupidest thing I've ever done."

Meylyne's throat tightened. All she had wanted was to make her mother happy, but she had messed it up—just like all those incantations she could never get right.

"Actually, this *trip* is the stupidest thing you've ever done. I'm telling you Meylyne—that queen of yours has gotta be nuts. You won't find a cure for the prince in the Valley of Half-Light. There is *nothing* good in the Valley of Half-Light."

"It wasn't Queen Emery—the Wise Well said I would find it there. And the Wise Well is never wrong," Meylyne insisted.

Blue looked skeptical but he let the topic drop.

"So, these First Rules that Glendoch has—what are the others?"

Ticking off her fingers, Meylyne answered, "No defiling nature, no eating Talking Animals, no unauthorized use of magic, and no trespassing between the worlds."

Blue thought for a minute. Then he grinned.

"So apart from not eating talking animals, breaking the other rules is pretty much *all* you're doing right now!"

Meylyne sunk her head in her hands.

"You no worry Meylyne," Hope said firmly. "Your intentions good. It all okay."

A family of beetles scuttled past their tent. Meylyne walked her fingers after them.

"I'm not so sure Queen Emery would agree with you," she muttered.

"Queen Emery afraid. We stallyinxes no trust her. Fear fuel bad decisions," Hope said.

"I don't trust her either," Meylyne replied vehemently. "She's always had it out for my mother and me. And it's not just because of Meph. *All* the royals hate alchemists."

Hope swished a fly off his rump with his tail.

"Not hate. Fear. Once royals *were* alchemists, remember?" He wriggled out of the makeshift tent. "Come on. Lunch over. Need get going again."

Meylyne groaned. She knew that moving would be agony. The salt from her sweat was acting like a double-duty torture machine with the sand on her chafed skin. Gritting her teeth, she crawled out from underneath her quilt, back into the blistering heat. A familiar twinge tickled her shoulder blades. Rummaging through her rucksack, she pulled out her bottle of pills and took one.

"What are those?" Blue asked.

"Allergy pills," she replied.

Blue stared at her as she continued gathering up her stuff. Then he shrugged and climbed up onto Hope's back. Meylyne climbed up behind him.

"People must think you're pretty cool back home," Blue shouted to her as Hope broke into a run. "You know, with your magic powers and Hearing skills and all that."

Meylyne laughed at him, and was rewarded with a mouthful of sand. She ducked her head under her sleeve.

"Please—no one thinks I'm cool. They just think I'm weird. If they notice me at all," she replied.

Blue was quiet for a minute. "Well, I don't think you're weird. I'd love to talk to nature and do magic and stuff!"

Meylyne wasn't sure what to make of this. It had never occurred to her that anyone would actually want what she had. For the next hour, they rode in silence. The bridge floated up toward two enormous sand dunes towering on either side. As they plodded through them, they were enveloped in a shimmery haze and a fine layer of dune-dust caused them to sparkle like gold. Then the bridge dipped down toward a forest of mandarin moss-birches and the air cooled to everyone's immense relief. A purple thicket rose up in between their trunks. Before long, thorns and brambles reached across the bridge, leaving only a few feet through which the three could pass.

As Hope slowed to a walk, Meylyne felt the hairs on her neck and arms prickle, and not just because the temperature had dropped. Her head swiveled from side to side.

Are we being watched?

She jumped as a twig cracked to the right. Blue took out his dagger, his knuckles white around its grip.

"Hate to say this, but I think we have company," he said quietly.

The silence pressed upon them as though it was alive. Then the air exploded with a deafening roar that Meylyne felt more than heard as a mass of fur, fangs and horns burst out of the shadows. She shrieked—

"It's a tusked lion!"

The beast paced before them, growling. His drool pooled on the ground. As big as Hope, his mane was full of brambles and his fur was streaked with gray. Two razor-sharp tusks jutted out of his head, streaked with what looked like dried blood.

"What you want, *Talking* Lion?" Hope demanded. "You can't attack us. We from Glendoch Proper—have treaty with you!"

The lion fixed his gaze on Meylyne. For a second she was aware of an awful emptiness in his eyes. Everything that happened next was a blur. The lion leapt out, hitting her like a boulder. Next she was on her back, pinned to the ground. There was a suffocating weight. Fangs at her throat. And then—

"Hey lion!"

Blue's voice sounded like he was miles away. There was a sudden movement. A flash of steel. The lion roared.

"Nggggg," Meylyne grunted as the colossal weight rolled off her.

"I wouldn't try that again," she heard Blue snarl.

There was a low growl, a crackling of twigs, and then silence.

Meylyne propped herself up on her elbows and peered around. There was no sign of the lion. Something nudged her shoulder and she looked up to find Hope staring at her.

"You okay?" he asked.

Hooking her arm around his neck, she pulled herself up and nodded, not quite able to speak.

Blue stood a few feet away, peering into the thicket. He held a sword in his hands.

"Lion's gone." He turned around, his mouth set in a grim line. "He won't get far with that wound though."

He trailed off, his brow furrowed.

"What is it, Blue?" Meylyne wheezed.

"I just remembered something that happened when my rival attacked me—a woman's voice. Something to do with 'wounding an enemy' . . ." His eyes widened. "A *woman's* voice. My rival was a *she!*"

"You remember what she look like?" Hope asked.

Blue shook his head and then peered back into the bushes. "No. And I can't believe I let that lion get away."

"Are you kidding?" Meylyne managed a smile. "You fought off a tusked lion Blue! You really *are* a warrior. Where did you get that sword from? And how on Glendoch could you even lift it? It's, like, twice your size!"

Blue grinned. "Yeah, how awesome is that? Watch—" With one, deft, movement, Blue turned his sword back to a dagger. "Ta-da—retractable blades! And I'll tell you something else—it's *really* sharp."

Just then, something rustled from within the thicket. Whirling around, Blue flicked his wrist and the dagger turned back into a sword. A raven flew out of the bushes. Hope and Meylyne breathed sighs of relief, but Blue remained tense.

"We need to keep moving. Too many places here for enemies to hide," he said. Staring at the bridge ahead, he pursed his lips, adding, "Where is *that* coming from?"

Tendrils of fog seeped out from the thicket.

"Must be ocean nearby," Hope replied, crouching down. "Blue right. We need keep moving. Get on."

Blue scrambled up onto his back. After a moment's hesitation, Meylyne climbed up after him. Her mind spun with questions.

"Why do you suppose that lion attacked us?"

"It was a lion. Why wouldn't it attack us?" Blue asked.

"Because Hope said he was a *Talking* Lion. Glendoch has a treaty with all Talking Animals—we don't eat them and they don't attack us!"

"How do you know he was a Talking Lion? He didn't say anything," Blue pointed out.

"We know our own," Hope replied.

Blue digested this before adding,

"I bet he was sent by my assassin."

Meylyne did not reply. Thinking about that chilled her to the bone, as did the fog that hung about them like wet cobwebs. Her teeth began to chatter as they moved deeper into the thicket. She strained to see through the mist but it was like trying to see through milk.

It's hiding something, she thought. *Is the lion here again?*

All her senses went on high alert.

No. Not the lion. Nothing that wants to hurt us, but definitely something.

Her knuckles whitened around Hope's mane as she tried to figure out what was lurking out there. The answer hovered at the edge of her mind but she could not latch onto it. By the time the fog cleared her nerves were as frayed as an old piece of string.

"Wow, we are *really* high up now," Blue said, making her jump. "Look!"

Peering over the edge of the bridge, Meylyne felt her

stomach lurch. They were *dizzyingly* high up. She couldn't even see the ground below them.

"Yes, and the bridge is really narrow now. What are those things growing on it?"

"Toadstools," Hope replied tersely.

Meylyne wrinkled her nose. The toadstools were big and yellow, and every now and then they emitted puffs of smoke that smelled like cheese. Meylyne cried out as Hope stepped on one and a thick cloud burst in his face, causing him to stumble.

"Sorry," he said. "You two get off. Safer that way. This terrain unfamiliar to me."

You have got to be joking, Meylyne thought as she and Blue slid off him. *This is safer? We don't stand a chance!*

At first, they trudged on in single file. Then, as the bridge got even narrower, Meylyne and Blue dropped to their hands and knees and crawled. There was a brief period of dusk before night fell—the deepest, blackest night they had ever known. The toadstools petered out and the air became fresh and salty. Fumbling in her rucksack, Meylyne pulled out a small, glowing bulb.

"What's that?" Blue asked.

"A Fiary," Meylyne replied, showing it to him.

Blue peered at the tiny creature flying frantically inside the bulb. "It looks like a fairy with its butt lit up."

"That's exactly what a Fiary is. They light up when they're captured like that."

"You're using a fairy as a flashlight?"

Meylyne ignored the indignation in his voice. To her relief, the ground had begun to spread out beneath them. It became soft and fuzzy as patches of moss sprung up. Soon the entire bridge was covered with moss so thick and soft she felt like she was crawling through a giant pillow. After a while she sat back on her heels.

"Can we stop now?" she asked, yawning. "I don't think I can go an inch further." She held up the Fiary and looked around. "It feels safe here. We can't roll off the edge of the bridge and there's no one around."

"We don't know that for sure," Blue said. "We can't see a thing beyond the piddly-little radius of your flashlight-fairy. I think we should take turns staying awake."

"Good idea. I stand guard first," Hope said.

Meylyne and Blue were more than happy to accept his offer and the three of them huddled together. The air closed around Meylyne like a giant sleeping bag.

This place is enchanted, she thought as her eyelids drooped shut. *I can feel it in the air.*

Within seconds, she was asleep.

When she awoke, the sky was brightening into a pinkish gold. Stretching, she breathed in the air that smelled like roses and lavender. Hope snored next to her. Despite his intentions, he had obviously fallen asleep. Propping herself up on her elbows, she gasped as her surroundings swam into view.

"Blue! Hope! Wake up!"

In a flash, Blue and Hope were on their feet, staring around in disbelief. They had woken up in a courtyard of moss-covered pavestones, surrounded by lemon trees. Marble fountains sprayed violet mist into the air.

And there, not more than fifteen feet away, was the biggest castle imaginable.

Its iridescent stone shimmered rose-gold in the dawn and its turrets rose up so high that their tops disappeared into the sky. If they'd kept going just a few minutes more last night, they would have run right into it. Its front door was inlaid with gems in the shape of a serpent that stared down at them from a great height.

Meylyne swallowed. *What could possibly need a door that big?*

She was suddenly aware of the sound of tiny bells, tinkling around her, and then the door flew open.

All three jumped back. At first nothing but a cavernous gloom reached out from the castle. Then a shape parted the shadows and a voice roared,

"FEE! FI! FO! FUM!"

9

Grimorex

WITH A FLICK OF HIS WRIST, BLUE'S DAGGER BECAME A sword. He moved in front of Meylyne and Hope, and the three of them backed away from the door. Ten seconds passed, and then twenty. When nothing happened, Meylyne squeaked out,

"I'm so sorry for trespassing. We . . . we didn't know where we were last night. I guess we'll just be off now!"

There was a roar of laughter and then a voice bellowed from inside—

"Oh that was *good!* You should see the looks on your faces. I've always wanted to do that 'fee fi' business."

Meylyne clutched Hope's mane as something that looked like an enormous stick insect stepped out into the light. It took her a second to realize it was actually some sort of man. As tall as a flagpole and just as thin, he looked like he'd been stretched by a machine to five times his normal length. The top of her head barely came up to his knees.

Her eyes traveled up his body. He wore pale blue, thigh-high boots, a yellow paisley waistcoat and a feathered cap. Bright blue eyes. Long brown hair. Pleasant face. A roguish twinkle entered into his eyes.

"It's from one of my *favorite* stories. Are you familiar with it?"

"Yes!" Blue blurted out. "I *am* familiar with it!" He elbowed Meylyne. "That's something else I remember!"

Meylyne ignored him. A memory had also stirred in her mind.

"Sir, are you . . . an *ogre?*"

The man threw back his head and guffawed again. "Of course I am! What—the height didn't give it away? You thought all ogres were beefy and toothless?"

Crossing his eyes, he hunched his back and let his tongue loll out of his mouth. "There—is that a bit more ogre-ish for you?"

Meylyne had no idea how to respond to this.

"Oh come now, cat got your tongues?" The ogre fished out a bon-bon from his waistcoat pocket. "Allow me to introduce myself. I am Grimorex. I trust you slept well—everyone always does on *my* land. It is full of enchantment."

All three cringed at the emphasis he put on the word *my.*

"Well, let's start with something easy. What are your names?" he asked, popping the bon-bon in his mouth.

Meylyne's stomach growled at the sight of his bulging cheek.

"I'm Meylyne. He's Hope. And he's Blue."

"Hmmm." Grimorex's gaze lingered on all three of them while he got a good look. "You all look ravenous. Let us break our fast together. Hope—I have a hot spring in the back, if you are so inclined. My fairies will bring whatever food you desire there."

Again there was the sound of bells tinkling. Looking

down, Meylyne gasped to see hundreds of fairies, no bigger than her thumbnail, emerge from the moss upon which they had laid all night.

"Fairies?" she breathed. "How beautiful! I've never seen so many—most Glendochian fairies left a long time ago."

"Of course they did. They lost all their rights when the New Order came in," Grimorex replied. Turning on his heel, he vanished back inside the gloom of his castle. "Come along!"

Blue made as if to follow him but Meylyne grabbed his arm.

"Where are you going? Let's make a run for it!"

"No point," Hope interjected. "We never escape his enchanted land."

"Says who? We could try!"

"Why? We about to get fed."

"Yes, and then *he'll* feed on us!"

Hope's face darkened.

"That stupid myth. Cause near extinction of ogres in Glendoch —"

"Can we stay on track here," Blue interrupted. "We have a hasty decision to make. Frankly, I'm with Hope. That dude is so thin, I doubt he eats anything, let alone humans. And I'm starved!"

Meylyne chewed her cheek while she weighed her own hunger against all the stories she'd heard about ogres. Meanwhile, Hope started to inch away.

"Wait —where are *you* going?" she hissed at him.

"Hot spring! We stallyinxes *love* hot spring."

"What? No! You can't split up from us!"

"Meylyne come *on*," Blue urged impatiently.

She turned around to find him waiting for her by Grimorex's massive front door.

"Why am I the only one with any sense around here? Just don't blame me when we're roasting on a spit."

Hurrying after Blue, Meylyne continued to grumble until they were both inside the castle. When their eyes adjusted to the gloom, they found themselves in a circular lobby. The walls were covered with gilded mirrors and tapestries that reminded Meylyne of the Between-World. A flight of stairs led off to the left, and to the right were three doors. One was ajar, light streaming through the crack.

"In here," Grimorex boomed. "I left the door open!"

The door was so heavy that Meylyne and Blue had to push together to open it. A blaze of sunlight assaulted their eyes. Squinting into it, they saw that this room had six sides, with windows so high they seemed to stretch past the sun.

"Sit!"

Grimorex motioned to a long oak table, lined with chairs on either side. The chairs loomed far above their heads.

"Um, how exactly?" asked Meylyne.

"Let me help you!"

Grimorex grasped her by the back of her cloak and swung her up onto a chair, stacked high with pillows. Blue was deposited onto the chair next to hers.

"I could've got up by myself," he grumbled.

Meylyne didn't answer him. She was too busy ogling the magnificent breakfast spread before them. There were baskets filled to the brim with orange cakes, cinnamon pastries, and crusty rolls; bowls brimming with large succulent grapes; platters of sausages and eggs; and large mugs of steaming hot chocolate. Despite her unease, her mouth began to water.

"Eat up!" Grimorex said, tying a napkin around his neck. "And please don't trouble your heads with all that nonsense about ogres eating humans. With all due respect, my palate is far more discerning than that. I suspect you both taste positively foul."

Meylyne eyed her pitchfork-sized fork.

"Do you mind if we use our fingers?"

"Yes I do."

Grimorex clapped his hands and two fairies flew over to Meylyne and Blue, carrying normal sized knives and forks.

"Apologies for not having those ready for you. Now please, dig in!"

For a moment there was silence while Meylyne and Blue heaped food onto their plates. Grimorex gulped down a pitcher of orange juice in one swallow.

"You're probably wondering why I live here so far from my own kind," he offered chattily.

"Yeah, 'at's what 'e were wondering," Blue mumbled, his cheeks bulging with cake.

Grimorex ignored Blue's sarcasm. "I did not grow up with the ogres, you see, I lived in a palace of tusked lions. Talking ones, that is."

Meylyne almost choked on her sausage. Tipping a barrel-sized cup toward her, she slurped down some hot chocolate.

"Tusked lions?" She wheezed. "So *you* set that lion on us!"

"What are you talking about?"

"The lion that tried to kill us!"

Grimorex peeled a grape. "First of all, I've no idea what you're talking about. Second of all, you're imagining things.

No Talking Animal would violate its treaty with Glendoch. Even when the Glendochian in question is not entirely normal." He scrutinized Meylyne. "What are you—one of those new Between-Worldian hybrids?"

Meylyne blinked. Her indignation at being told she was imagining things *and* not normal battled with her surprise that he knew what she was.

"Yes," she replied stiffly. "A garloch. I'm one of those. How did you know?"

Grimorex clapped his hands.

"I knew it! You're the first one I've met. I can always tell where a person is from. Apart from you—"

Now he squinted at Blue. "If I didn't know better, I'd say you were not of *this* world at all."

Blue put down the roll he was gnawing.

"Where am I from then?"

Grimorex was silent for a moment. Then he shook his head. "It's not possible. The tunnels between our worlds disappeared a long time ago."

"What world?"

"No matter, I am mistaken. Now," he turned his attention back to Meylyne. "Do tell me of the gossip in Glendoch Proper. Anything interesting going on in the courts?"

"Wait a minute," Blue protested. "Tell me where you think I'm from!"

Grimorex held up his hand in front of Blue's face.

"I assure you, I'm mistaken." He bent in closer to Meylyne. "Is Meph still up to his shenanigans?"

Meylyne froze. The food in her mouth suddenly tasted like sawdust.

"You've heard of Meph all the way out here?" she asked.

Grimorex dabbed his upper lip with a napkin. A shifty look entered into his eyes.

"Indeed I have."

Meylyne swallowed her mouthful with difficulty. It seemed there was no escaping her father's notoriety.

Grimorex popped a plum in his mouth, adding,

"It is odd, is it not, that in recent years he would choose only one half of your citizens to wreak havoc upon? At least with the Cabbage-Wind he targeted *all* Glendochians."

Meylyne put down her knife and fork. "If you don't mind my asking, *how* do you know all this? Our news-scrolls don't leave our borders."

"What's the Cabbage-Wind?" Blue piped up.

Licking his lips, Grimorex did not reply to either question. He had the look of someone with a delicious secret that he was dying to share. One of his fairies flew to him and hovered by his ear, tinkling something. As the fairy flew off, she giggled, adding, "And you might want to offer them a bath, when you're finished!"

Meylyne flushed.

"I heard that," she shouted at the fairy. "It's not like I've had the opportunity to bathe these last few days!"

"You understood my fairy?" Grimorex stared at her. "But that means you're a Hearer. Are all Garloch's Hearers?"

"I don't know. I'm the only one I know," Meylyne replied.

Grimorex tapped his nose.

"Of course, it could be from your *Garlysle* blood that you inherited your Hearing powers. Not that there are many Garlysles that can still Hear. Other than Meph, I know of none."

Meylyne's face got even redder.

"Yeah well, that's her dad," Blue interjected. "Ow! What did you do that for?"

Meylyne had kicked him under the table. Grimorex looked from her, to Blue, and back to Meylyne. His eyes bulged out of his head.

"You're Meph's *daughter*?"

"Now look what you've done," Meylyne hissed at Blue.

Grimorex leaned back in his chair.

"My, my. Meph's daughter, at my table."

Meylyne scowled at him. "It's not like I can help who my father is."

Grimorex got a weird look on his face, like he was remembering something happy and sad at the same time.

"What *exactly* are you doing here?" he asked her. "You must have good reason for breaking one of Glendoch's First rules."

"Actually she's breaking a bunch of them," Blue chortled. "Ow! Enough with the kicking already!"

"We're here by accident," Meylyne said, glaring at Blue. "We were trying to get to the Valley of Half-Light, but we went the wrong way and we ended up here instead."

"You were going to the Valley of Half-Light? On *purpose?*" said Grimorex.

"That's what I said! She's got this half-baked notion that she'll find a cure for some prince there," Blue said.

"A cure for Prince Piam's aging disease?" Grimorex snorted. "Well now that is half-baked! It doesn't exist. Many have tried and failed in that regard. Including your mother!"

Meylyne folded her arms.

"How do you *know* all this?"

Grimorex waved his hand. "I'll tell you that later. First tell me *your* story. Why have you embarked on this exercise in futility?"

Meylyne pressed her lips together and did not reply.

"Look, you won't get to the Valley of Half-Light without my help, trust me. The road leading to it is covered with sucking mud, scorpions, and poison-spitting pustules. It's almost as bad as the valley itself!"

"Covered with *what?*" Meylyne screeched. "No, don't say it again," she snapped as Grimorex began to repeat himself. Tears pricked her eyes. She would never get to the Valley of Half-Light at this rate.

Leaning over, Grimorex covered her hand with his.

"I promise, I can help you. But you have to tell me more."

"Why should I? You know far too much about Glendoch—you're obviously keeping secrets from *us!*"

"That doesn't mean I'm not on your side."

Meylyne gave Grimorex a hard look. Deep down, she wanted to trust him.

"Fine," she muttered. "Here's the deal—I trespassed in the Above-World, and got caught, so Queen Emery told my mother she'd have to cure Prince Piam to earn my pardon—"

"You forgot the bit where you squashed him," Blue interjected, scooting out of reach of her foot.

"—but the Wise Well told me *I* had to cure him and that I'd find the cure in the Valley of Half-Light." She sat back. "End of story."

"No, I'd say that's the *beginning* of the story." Grimorex exhaled slowly. "I'm telling you, you won't find the cure you seek in the Valley of Half-Light. But if the *Wise Well* told you to go there, then by Jove we must get you there!"

Meylyne jumped as he leapt to his feet and scooped her up in one hand.

"Whoa—where are we going?"

Grimorex ignored her. Grabbing Blue in the other hand, he bounded down a long, narrow hallway and out into the back garden. Drifts of forget-me-nots and daffodils and huge azaleas surrounded them and off to the right a crop of silver-birches swayed in the breeze. Grimorex wound his way between the trees, dodging thick strands of white moss hanging from their branches.

"There!" Grimorex said, depositing Meylyne and Blue on the ground. "What do you think of that?"

Steadying themselves, Meylyne and Blue found that they stood before an emerald-green lagoon, so clear they could see all the way to the bottom. Neither said a word. It was not, however, the lagoon that rendered them speechless.

It was that which lay inside.

10

The Fallen Guardian

A GIGANTIC CHARIOT BLAZED BEFORE THEM. GLITTERING in the morning sunlight, it appeared to be made entirely of crystal. A formidable creature, also crystal, was attached to its shaft. Half-woman, half-dragon, she stared into the distance; pride and ferocity mingling in her sparkling face. She almost looked alive.

"Wow," Blue breathed, shielding his eyes. "What is that—some sort of glass wagon?"

"Oh no," Grimorex replied softly. "That is a *chariot*—an enchanted, flying, *diamond* chariot, no less."

"That huge thing is a *diamond?* I don't believe you!"

Grimorex shot Blue a scornful look. "Trust me child. I know my diamonds. Admittedly this—" he returned his gaze to the chariot, "—is by the far the most magnificent I have ever seen. Of all my toys, she is the best! She knows *everywhere* there is. We have been to places you could not even *dream* existed!"

He snapped his fingers and the chariot rolled out of the lagoon toward them, water streaming off its wheels. Grimorex flicked a latch and the back swung open. "Please, climb aboard!"

Blue could barely see over the chariot floor. With a flying leap, he hoisted himself inside.

"Blue wait!" Meylyne cried, peering inside. Multi-colored lights criss-crossed before her, blurring Blue's shape as he disappeared toward the front of the chariot.

"Blue, will you *please* come back here!" Meylyne shouted.

"No, you come here!"

Meylyne chewed her lip. She felt drawn to the chariot and afraid of it at the same time.

"She can take you where you *need* to go, not necessarily where you *want* to go," Grimorex explained, as if reading her mind. "Hop on now!"

Meylyne's curiosity got the better of her. Stepping aboard, she was instantly immersed in a dazzling array of light and color. The chariot's sides sloped up above her as she walked toward the front, trailing her hands along the sparkling alcoves that had been cut into them and lined with cushions, perfect for sitting on. The bottom was so smooth and clear it was almost invisible. Looking down, Meylyne saw clown-fish and pearl-eels peeping up at her. Something about the chariot seemed familiar to her, but she couldn't figure out what. Feeling someone at her side, she turned and felt a rush of relief to see that it was Hope.

"Hi Hope! How'd you find us?"

But before Hope could reply, Grimorex shouted, "Brace yourselves!"

Meylyne grabbed Hope as the dragon-lady unfurled her wings in stiff, mechanical jerks. The chariot rose up out of the lake, water streaming from its sides and then whisked off, so fast that Meylyne and Hope flew backward, landing in the

alcoves. Blue ended up a few rows behin
into an alcove of his own. Pulling himself
iot's knobby bits, he crawled over and pl
the alcove behind Meylyne's.

"This is *great*," he said, beaming. "Hey Hope!"

Hope nodded at him. Judging by the expression on his face, he did not share Blue's enthusiasm for flying-diamond-chariot travel. Clambering to her feet, a thrill of excitement surged through Meylyne as she stared into the wind rushing at them. It made her skin tingle and her eyes water. A few seconds later, Hope stood at her side with Blue on his back. His thick mane streamed behind them like liquid charcoal.

"This is *awesome!*" Blue cried. "We're really flying!"

"I know! This is like . . . the *opposite* of the Between-World!" Meylyne laughed.

A vast ocean shimmered below them. Meylyne could just about make out the bridge above it. It stretched for miles, disappearing over the horizon. Glendoch was nowhere in sight.

"That Marzappan Sea beneath us. That mean Grimorex live in Celadonia. How we come so far in one night?" Hope asked.

Meylyne frowned. Celadonia was *very* far from Glendoch. "We couldn't, unless sorcery was involved."

"Sorcery? Whose? *You* didn't magic us anywhere!" Blue pointed out.

"I have no idea. We obviously went the wrong way when the bridge split. Maybe we entered a grytch."

"What's that?" asked Blue.

Meylyne scrunched up her brow. Grytches were tricky to describe.

"It's a bit like a tunnel. Back when Glendoch was really enchanted, it used to have these places that, when you enter them, you get transported really quickly to somewhere else. Supposedly they make you feel like you've been chewed up and spat out the other end—"

"Which we didn't," Blue pointed out.

"I know, but it's the only thing I can think of for how we got all the way to Celadonia in one night."

The three fell into silence as the chariot flew steadily onward. To the ships below it looked like a giant prism as it hurtled past the sun. Then it disappeared into a swirling cloudbank and Meylyne, Hope and Blue were engulfed in white mist. They were drenched in minutes. Hope settled himself into an alcove while Blue explored the rest of the chariot.

Meylyne stayed where she was. The wetness didn't bother her. If anything, she felt clean for the first time in days. Closing her eyes, she heard the clouds whispering about the sea—they spoke of mermaids and whirlpools and channels to distant worlds.

Finally the clouds thinned and slivers of blue emerged. Glendoch was in sight now. Meylyne could see its golden Titons and silver-white mountains; the six cities just beyond. As they drew nearer, the chariot dipped down until Meylyne could see the bridge upon which they had traveled quite clearly.

"Blue, Hope, look—I can see where the bridge split!"

Blue dashed over and scrambled up onto Hope's back.

"Oh yeah! It looks like a piece of string all knotted up."

"Bridge look weird. Can chariot go lower?" Hope asked.

"It does look weird," Meylyne agreed as the chariot veered downward. "It's as if the ground is moving."

As they dropped even lower, Meylyne realized that the bridge was not moving but covered in scorpions crawling over one another. The bridge also had red patches on it, which the scorpions seemed careful to avoid. The patches oozed yellow liquid and when a scorpion came too close, the red patch would spit at it. Then the scorpion rolled onto its back, writhing before going still.

"*Yeech!*" Meylyne said. "I suppose we should be thankful that we went the wrong way!"

Before anyone could reply, the chariot whizzed off to the right and bumped to a halt. All around them were branches and leaves. Blue peered through the foliage, and then ducked down into an alcove.

"We're here!" he hissed. "See that foggy-looking valley? That's the Valley of Half-Light!"

Meylyne's stomach lurched and she ducked down so that only her eyes showed above the chariot. Looking to where Blue pointed, she saw a lush green valley with tendrils of mist rising out of it.

"*That's* the Valley of Half-Light?" she whispered in disbelief. "It looks so ordinary. Pretty, even."

It was hard to equate this place with the vortex of evil she had heard it was. She sat down beside Blue. All the color had drained from his face.

"Um, do those spher things ever leave the Valley? Because we're kinda close," he said.

"Don't worry. They can't leave—they're trapped inside the Valley by the Great Oaken Mother," Meylyne said.

Blue frowned in confusion.

"Enchanted tree," Hope explained.

"Enchanted tree?" Blue echoed. Then he sighed. "Of course it is. So now what do we do?"

Meylyne blinked. "I don't know. The Well said that 'everything I needed to know' would be revealed to me along the way. But *nothing* has been revealed—"

"Ssshh!" Hope interrupted. "Hear that?"

At first, Meylyne heard nothing. Then a moaning sound rose up around her and a chill snaked up her spine.

"Yes. What *is* that?" she whispered.

"I don't hear anything," said Blue.

"Noise come from Tree," Hope said.

The tree? Reaching up, Meylyne touched one of the tree's leaves, which was brown and mottled. The tree moaned again, sounding so full of pain that Meylyne's breath caught in her throat.

"What's the matter?" she asked the tree.

At first there was silence. Then a barely audible whisper.

"Poisoned. Failing Glendoch."

"Failing Glendoch?" Meylyne echoed. "What do you mean?"

More silence. Then,

"I am the Great Oaken Mother."

Meylyne gasped in disbelief, taking stock of the tree for the first time. It was clearly dying—its bark was flaking off in dusty chunks and its leaves shredded and drooping. She could feel its branches groaning under the chariot's weight.

"We have to move, chariot. This tree is really sick," she urged.

The chariot immediately lifted from its perch and landed on the ground nearby. Meylyne and Hope locked eyes.

"This can't be happening," Meylyne murmured.

"What's the deal?" Blue asked nervously.

"The deal is that this tree is the Great Oaken Mother we just told you about," Meylyne replied, her tone desperate. "It's her powers that stop the sphers from escaping the Valley of Half-Light and she's been poisoned! She's supposed to live forever. If she dies, the sphers can get out!"

"Maybe some already have," Hope said grimly. "Remember lion?"

Meylyne recalled the emptiness in the tusked lion's eyes.

"Of course! That would explain why he attacked us!"

"Whoa! You mean to tell me that those sphers are *not* trapped inside the Valley of Half-Light?" Blue's voice rose a notch. "Let's get outta here!"

Hope sniffed the air.

"No worry. No sphers here. Must be because tree still alive. Suspect most sphers still inside Valley. For now."

"But *why?* Who would poison the Great Oaken Mother? Who could possibly want the sphers escaping?" Meylyne asked.

"No idea. We need ask Tree," Hope replied.

"Hope wait!" Meylyne hissed as he slunk out of the chariot and padded toward the tree.

Hope continued to walk away. Blue grasped her hand.

"Come on, we have to go with him."

Judging by the quiver in his voice, Blue was just as scared as she was. Together, they jumped out of the chariot and caught up to Hope, wrinkling their noses at the sickly-sweet smell of rotting fruit. With one eye on the valley beyond, Meylyne put her hand on the tree's trunk. A piece of bark fell to the ground.

"Poor tree. Who did this to you?" she murmured.

The tree sighed, struggling to answer. It appeared to be losing strength by the second. It whispered something but Meylyne could not tell what it said.

"Pardon?"

She pressed her ear against the tree's trunk, grimacing as the stench filled her nostrils. This time she could just about make out what the tree said.

"What did it say?" Blue demanded as she pulled away.

"It sounded like, 'the Thorn Queen,' but I can't be sure."

The tree shook its branches, showering them with dead leaves. "Fetch Trisdyan," it rasped. "He can cure me."

Before Meylyne could reply, Hope froze.

"Look!"

A wisp of smoke inched its way toward them.

"Back to chariot," Hope ordered. "Now!"

Meylyne and Blue did not need to be told twice. Running faster than they had ever done before, they reached the chariot in seconds.

"Fly, chariot—anywhere!" Meylyne screamed once they were all inside.

The chariot shot away, once again catapulting the three into its alcoves. Meylyne crawled over to Hope and Blue, shaking like jelly.

"Uggghhhh! That was a spher, wasn't it?" she asked.

Hugging his knees, Blue nodded. Then he scrambled to his feet and ran to the other side of the chariot, retching.

Meylyne felt sick too. A memory had roused itself in her mind.

"You know Hope, before I left, Queen Emery said her

queendom was close to war. At the time I thought she was just crazy but maybe she was right."

"What you mean?"

"Well if some sphers *have* escaped and infected Glendochians then those Glendochians would turn on one another, wouldn't they? And if enough people got involved, wouldn't that be a war?"

Hope looked grave as he nodded.

"We must save Great Oaken Mother. Or no point in returning home. No home to return to."

11

Grimorex has an Idea

MEYLYNE SHIVERED AS HOPE'S WORDS ECHOED IN HER MIND.

No home to return to.

He was right. Only two fates awaited those infected by sphers—the Shadow Cellars and death. Blue plopped down next to them. His face was blotchy and he was trembling.

"Are you okay?" Meylyne asked him.

Blue nodded curtly. "What were you saying about war?"

"Nothing," Meylyne replied, not wanting to think about that any more. "Listen—the Great Oaken Mother told me to fetch Trisdyan—that *he* could help her."

"Who's Trisdyan?" Blue asked.

Pulling herself up, Meylyne peered over the chariot's side and sighed. The air was crystal clear. In the distance, Glendoch's white-capped mountains were fading away.

"No one really knows. The Above-Worldians—" she stole a glance at Hope "—that is the Above-Worldian *humans* think he's just a myth. The Between-Worldians don't think that though."

"Nor us," Hope interjected.

"Yes but who is he?" Blue pressed.

"I'm getting there! According to legend, he's a wizard of

the oldest order. He's the one that infused the Great Oaken Mother with the power to guard the sphers. But no one has ever seen him."

"Fat lot of good that does us then." Blue chewed his lip. "You said that the Tree Mother said the Thorn Queen did this to her, right?"

"Yes, but I have no idea who that is! I suppose we can ask Grimorex when we see him."

"I have idea," Hope replied. "Remember story about Queen Emery—when she forced to drink broth of thorns?"

"Of course!" Meylyne exclaimed. "For getting Princess Amber kidnapped. Why didn't I think of that?"

"Well, no make sense. Why Queen Emery destroy her own Queendom?"

"Sorry. Kinda lost here. Who is Princess Amber?" Blue asked.

A cloud passed over the sun, casting a shadow over them. Meylyne felt her stomach tighten the way it always did when her thoughts dwelled on Princess Amber. Of all the things her father had done, this was possibly his worst.

"Princess Amber was Queen Emery's best friend. Only Queen Emery got her kidnapped so she could rule all Glendoch by herself."

And it was all my father's fault.

"That rumor," Hope said sharply. "Amber get kidnapped and everyone blame Emery for it. Make her drink thorns as punishment. *That* part true."

"Oh." Blue still looked puzzled. "So, you usually have *two* queens ruling Glendoch?"

"Yes—well kings or queens. The House of Cardinal— that's

Queen Emery's house—rules the city of Tyr and the House of Rose is 'sposed to rule the other Glendochian cities. They're called the Francescan cities for short. But the Roses can't seem to choose another ruler in Princess Amber's place, so Queen Emery rules the whole thing."

"And not very well," Hope added. "That why Tyrians and Francescans fight. Francescans feel unprotected. Meph attack them and Queen Emery can't help."

"Hmmm." Blue thought for a minute. "And why is Queen Emery blamed for the other one's kidnap?"

"Cabbage-Wind," Hope replied.

Blue gave Hope a blank look and he stared pointedly at Meylyne but she turned away. She wasn't going to tell Blue. The shame of it was like a burning thread in her throat.

Hope sighed.

"Cabbage-Wind rumored to be dragon's breath," he explained. "But everyone believes Meph put dragon up to it. One night, fifteen years past—"

"Thirteen," Meylyne muttered.

"*Thirteen* years past," Hope continued, "wind slithered down from Glendoch's peak—no ordinary wind. More like snake! It slither through Glendoch's cities; crack window panes and freeze wells. Anyone caught in it suffer strange maladies. Ears turn black . . . hands turn into cabbages . . . some warble like marsh-frogs. And these *lucky* ones! Others look fine but they start behave nasty. No one know, but their *hearts* turn into cabbages—rotten ones!"

"Geez!" Blue exclaimed.

"And rottenness of hearts cause them commit crimes normally not done—some crimes against nature get them imprisoned in the Between-World. They become known as Cabbage-Windians."

"I see." Blue mulled this over for a minute. "But what does that have to do with Princess Amber being kidnapped?"

"Day after Cabbage-Wind, princesses walk to top of Glendoch Mountain. Not realize Princess Emery's heart a cabbage! When near top, she pluck sacred flower—punishable by imprisonment by garlysle law. Princess Amber snatch from her, meaning to re-plant, but garlysle burst out of ice and drag her down to Between-World."

"I see," Blue said. "And is that when all the fighting between the two sides of Glendoch began?"

"Yes," Meylyne replied. "And it's all my father's fault. Even after the physicians worked out what had happened and my Great-Uncle ordered the release of the Cabbage-Windians, Princess Amber was never found."

The shame of it weighed upon her like a pile of rocks in her tummy. From the whispers of her classmates to the deliberate avoidance from the shop-keepers down the street, she had felt the blame for this particular act of her father's madness ever since she could remember.

Blue nodded, his brow furrowed. "Well it still doesn't make sense. Hope's right—why would Queen Emery destroy her own Queendom now?"

Meylyne had no good answer for him. She lapsed into silence, staring morosely at the blue-green sea that stretched below them for miles and miles. *Maybe Queen Emery's as crazy as my father—so intent on killing him that she'll do anything—even start a war.*

She did not feel the prickle in her shoulder blades at first. When it came again, more like a bee sting this time, she was jolted out of her worrisome thoughts. Pulling out her pills, she swallowed one, trying not to let Hope and Blue see. She could feel Hope's eyes boring into her back.

I could just tell them. Neither of them would care about my secret.

She kept quiet. This was not the right time for spilling secrets. Closing her eyes, she tried to silence her mind so that the clouds might speak to her again. They would surely know who the Thorn Queen was. The clouds however remained silent, and eventually a smudge appeared on the horizon.

"That place where Grimorex lives, what's it called again?" Blue shouted above the wind.

"Celadonia. I don't know much about it. We never get visitors aside from the merchants—and they aren't allowed beyond the harbors," Meylyne replied.

The chariot picked up speed and soon the edges of Celadonia came into view. To the north, Meylyne saw white-capped mountains and a sharp glint of light. Grimorex's castle loomed straight ahead of them. As it got nearer and nearer, Meylyne's palms began to sweat. If they didn't slow down they would crash right into it! Then the chariot plunged downward and she shrieked as she catapaulted to the back of the chariot along with Hope and Blue.

"Slow down!" she screamed.

Just as she was certain they would crash into the lagoon, the chariot pulled up, skimming across the top of the water and bumping to a stop, inches from the shore. Meylyne, Hope, and Blue lay in a sprawled heap on the floor. They were all silently congratulating themselves on being alive when an enormous shadow loomed over them.

"Hello my friends!" Grimorex's face was wreathed in

smiles as he stared down at them. A blue and green striped bow tie bobbed up and down on his neck. "How delightful to see you so soon. I trust you were successful?"

His smile vanished as Meylyne pushed herself up, using Blue's soggy head for support. They had each got drenched from the spray.

"You look a tad peaked, all of you. Well, I did try to warn you. No one ventures inside the Valley of Half-Light voluntarily. The sphers are not to be trifled with—"

"We never made it inside the Valley," Meylyne cut him off. "The Great Oaken Mother has been poisoned. Sphers are escaping."

Grimorex fell silent, his mouth open. He blinked three times and when he spoke again his tone had no trace of its usual lightness.

"*Poisoned?* You're sure of this?"

Meylyne nodded. "The tree said the Thorn Queen had done it."

Grimorex frowned. Opening the back of the chariot, he walked away.

"Come," he called over his shoulder.

Scrambling out of the chariot, Meylyne, Hope, and Blue followed Grimorex as he wandered down the mossy path. This time they turned away from the castle, winding their way through a lemon orchard to end up at a jasmine-covered gazebo. Inside a picnic table was set with a silver teapot and an assortment of doughnuts.

"Help yourselves," Grimorex said, picking up Meylyne and Blue and depositing them on the table. "Sorry, Hope. Not much to interest you here."

Grimorex sat down and stared at Meylyne.

"You say the Great Oaken Mother said that the *Thorn Queen* did this to her?"

"Yes, do you know who that is?" she asked.

Grimorex stroked his chin. "An old rumor comes to mind. You must have heard it—that when Queen Emery was a girl she was forced to drink a broth of thorns as penance for what she did to Princess Amber."

"Yes! That's what we thought at first, but it doesn't make sense. Why would Queen Emery destroy her own Queendom?"

"Why indeed?" Grimorex murmured, lapsing into silence.

For a moment all that could be heard was the sound of crickets chirping and Blue munching on a donut. The scent of roses permeated the air.

"More important question—how save Great Oaken Mother?" Hope said to Grimorex. "She said need Trisdyan."

Grimorex sneezed and peered up at the sky that had become violet in the twilight.

"All Glendoch needs Trisdyan," he replied wistfully. "Alas he is nowhere to be found."

"Yeah we covered that already. So what can we do?" Blue asked impatiently.

A twig cracked from beyond the orchard. Looking toward the noise, Meylyne thought she saw something move behind a tree. In a flash, Grimorex dashed to where the noise had come from.

"Ugh! A snake!" he said.

Walking back to the table, he scooped up Meylyne and Blue and strode back to his castle. "Let's go inside. I can't abide snakes and it's getting chilly out here."

They entered the castle through a door that led them into an enormous kitchen in which an army of fairies prepared supper. Some chopped vegetables and spices while others rolled out a large circle of dough. A delicious assortment of scents filled the air. Grimorex threaded his way through all this activity to a spiral staircase at the back.

"We shall eat in my study," he announced, climbing the staircase.

When he reached the top, he flicked a light switch and two lamps came on, revealing a room with pink and gold striped wallpaper and a fireplace in the corner. Three of the walls were lined with books, while the fourth was all glass. Meylyne walked over to it, almost tripping over a huge white tiger stretched out on the floor. It didn't move.

"Pay no attention to Opholo," Grimorex said. "She's sound asleep."

To his right was a black-and-gold lacquered sideboard with a decanter and a set of crystal goblets on top. Pouring three glasses, he handed one to Meylyne and one to Blue.

"I sometimes prefer to eat supper here. Far cozier than the dining room." He held up his glass. "Cheers!"

Meylyne took a sip of her drink. It tasted of cinnamon and burned her throat going down. A feeling of lightness stole over her, as if she was suspended in air. She set her goblet on a bookshelf.

"What are we going to do?" she asked, echoing Blue's earlier question.

Kneeling before the fireplace, Grimorex set the logs aflame and then sat down in an armchair. Meylyne, Blue, and Hope sat down on the rug that was so plush it felt like a bed.

"Do you remember I told you that I grew up in the Palace of Lions? Well, as it happens, the lions and the eagles are old friends. I heard of an eagle that is a direct descendant from the Parliament of Thor-Schael. It is said that his feathers are suffused with extraordinary power," Grimorex said.

Blue grimaced as he took a swig of his drink. "What's the Parliament of Thor-Schael?"

"Do you know of Trisdyan?"

Blue's eyes began to water from the drink. "Old wizard," he wheezed.

Grimorex looked at Blue as if he'd just vomited on his favorite pair of trousers.

"Trisdyan is *far* more than an old wizard! It was he that summoned the Original Six when the old Glendoch began to die. He that harnesses the powers of good when the powers of evil start to rise—"

Grimorex's voice had also started to rise. With a deep breath, he brought it back down.

"And the Parliament of Thor-Schael are his trusted cohorts."

"I still have no idea what you're talking about," Blue replied impatiently.

"I'm talking about using one of the eagle's feathers to heal the Great Oaken Mother."

Meylyne folded her arms. "You're kidding right? We're going to use a *feather* to save Glendoch?"

Grimorex drained his drink in one gulp. "Do you have a better plan?"

"Yes! I'm going to go back home, fetch my mother, and *she* will heal the Great Oaken Mother!"

"Doubtful. Trisdyan himself fortified the Great Oaken

Mother against all foes. If someone has found a way to poison her, then we will need something of Trisdyan's power to heal her."

"I'm sure my mother can do it," Meylyne insisted.

Grimorex regarded her. "What makes you so sure? She can't heal Prince Piam of his rapid-aging affliction. And why not? It can't be that difficult—not for a powerful sorceress like your mother. The little I know of alchemy tells me that if Prince Piam's disease were of *this* world, your mother could cure him."

Meylyne threw up her arms. "Who cares about him now? Glendoch being overrun by sphers is a lot more important than some stupid prince's disease!"

Grimorex got up and poured himself another drink.

"Not necessarily. What if both have the same culprit at their source?"

Meylyne stared at Grimorex, waiting for him to say more but instead he pulled a cord on the wall. A distant clanging was heard and the white tiger woke up. Rising to her feet, she surveyed the room, and then padded out of it. Grimorex followed her to the door and said,

"After supper, I shall show you something—something that I think may offer us a clue as to the source of both your prince's disease and the Great Oaken Mother's demise. But for now, we eat!"

12

The Secret of the Diamond Chariot

TWO HOURS LATER, MEYLYNE AND BLUE LAY BACK IN their chairs. Grimorex's fairies had made a huge pie for supper that was stuffed with sweet potatoes smothered in gravy and spices they had never tasted before. Dessert was another pie; this one stuffed with hot gooey apples and custard bubbling over the sides. They had devoured every last crumb and now they felt as though they might burst. When the last plate had been cleared away, Grimorex pulled on a mauve smoking jacket and lit a pipe.

"No falling asleep young lady," he said to Meylyne between puffs. "There is something I still need to show you!"

Meylyne struggled to keep her eyes open. "Really?" she yawned. "It can't wait until morning?"

"Cover your mouth please. And no it can't wait. We need to set off at the break of dawn, if we are to make it to the Palace of Lions by dusk."

That woke Meylyne up.

"The Palace of Lions? What are you talking about?"

"I told you before—the lions will know the whereabouts of the eagle we must find."

Meylyne rolled her eyes.

"Look, this eagle *can't* exist. If it did, I'd have heard of it. *Everyone* would want one of its feathers! I just want to go to bed now."

Clamping his pipe between his teeth, Grimorex picked up Meylyne and Blue, one in each hand.

"Trust me, you won't be tired when you see what I have to show you!" Glancing behind him, he gestured at Hope to follow them. "You too!"

Grimorex ignored Meylyne's protests as he made his way down the spiral staircase, through the kitchen still buzzing with fairies cleaning up, and into the garden.

The outside was blanketed in silence. Trees and flowers glowed frostily in the moon's silver light, and as they headed into the forest, glowing fireflies dotted the air. Within a few minutes they were back at the diamond chariot.

As grumpy as Meylyne was, she had to admit that it looked even more magnificent than before. The moonlight set the diamonds ablaze, bathing them all in rippling patterns of silver and blue.

Grimorex climbed inside. Depositing Meylyne and Blue on a cushion, he made his way to the front of his chariot. There was a mysterious smile on his face when he turned around.

Meylyne scowled back at him.

"Can we get on with this please? I know we have to save Glendoch and everything but I'm tired and cold and I want to go to bed!"

Grimorex rested his hand on what looked like a lever.

"Don't worry, you'll be warm and wide awake in a minute. You had asked, earlier, how it was that I know so much about Glendoch. Well here, my dear—" Grimorex pulled down the lever. "Is the answer—"

All of a sudden, the air in front of Meylyne and Blue began to wobble. Then it whirled around like a funnel, crackling and popping with sparks flying out. Meylyne tried to scoot back and ended up falling off the pillow.

"Whoa!" Blue gasped. "What's going on?"

Grimorex trained his eyes on the air-funnel. "Old Glendoch. Second Monday, Month of the Flowers, Year of the Star."

As Meylyne scrambled to her feet, shapes emerged from within the whirling air and a beautiful scene came into focus—a sparkling ice-mountain, dotted with firs and a stream coursing down from the top, rainbow-colored fish jumping from its water. At the bottom, a family of ogres and two garlysles sat around a fire and to their right three stallyinxes sat in a steamy, glacial pool.

"You see," Grimorex announced triumphantly. "This is the chariot's most prized trick! *She can show you Glendoch's past!*"

Meylyne, Hope, and Blue gazed, spellbound, into the whirling air funnel.

"No way," Meylyne breathed. "So *that's* how you know so much about Glendoch!"

"Indeed it is."

For a moment, no one said a word. Meylyne could not believe she was looking at the same Glendoch in which she'd grown up. She thought about the date Grimorex had said and calculated that this scene was about a thousand years old. Aside from Glendoch Mountain, it looked entirely different. Garlysles sitting side-by-side with the stallyinxes. No cities. No humans.

"Why is the air tinged with gold?" she asked.

"Alchemy," Grimorex replied softly.

Meylyne's eyes got even wider.

Alchemy? So much you can see it in the air?

As Meylyne gazed in awe at the scene before her, something niggled at her. She was reminded of something but could not remember what.

"That's awesome!" Blue burst out. "We can ask the chariot to show us who poisoned the Great Oaken Mother, right?"

"Unfortunately not," Grimorex replied. "You have to ask for a specific date. It would take us *years* to go through all the possible days upon which that travesty occurred."

"Well we'll just go back to the tree and ask it when it happened then," Blue said.

"That won't work. Nature does not see time. Everything happens in the now. Do you want to see more?"

"Wait!"

Meylyne had remembered what it was that niggled her. Dumping her rucksack on the ground, she rummaged through it, muttering,

"I *knew* something about the chariot looked familiar— look!"

She pulled out her hand from her rucksack, holding up her mother's crystal for everyone to see.

"What is that?" Grimorex asked, squinting at it.

"It's my mother's enchanted crystal. She uses it, or rather she *used* it before I stole it from her to see what was going on in Glendoch. Doesn't it look like a piece of the chariot?"

Grimorex held out his hand. "May I?"

Meylyne handed him the crystal and he inspected it thoroughly, murmuring,

"That is no crystal, my child. It is undoubtedly a diamond. And yes—definitely from the same diamond from which the chariot was hewn, if not from the chariot itself! How did your mother come by this?"

"I've no idea. It's different from the chariot though. It doesn't show Glendoch's past; it shows what's going on in Glendoch right now."

Blue's eyes lit up to hear this. "Really? Well let's fire it up then! I wanna see what's going on in Glendoch right now!"

Meylyne bit her lip. Her mother would kill her if she found out that not only had she taken her diamond-crystal but that she had used it too.

"It'll be boring. It's night time—everyone will be asleep and besides, Grimorex has something else to show us, right Grimorex?"

"That's all right, it can wait. Even at night time in Glendoch, there is bound to be something of interest going on."

Grimorex's voice oozed curiosity. Obviously he too was dying to see what was happening in Glendoch right now. *As are you,* a voice whispered in her head. *And you're in so much trouble anyway. Who cares if you do something else wrong?*

She exhaled. "Okay. But only for a minute!"

With a tingle of excitement, she moved her fingers across the diamond-crystal and whispered the password to turn it on. In a flash, the diamond lit up, filling with swirling colors.

"Between-World, my cave," she said.

The colors parted to reveal the rich, reddish-orange walls of her tunnel and the door to her cave.

"Inside," she added.

The colors swirled again and her living room emerged. Meylyne's throat tightened. She never thought she could miss that ugly couch and even uglier painting so badly.

"Mother's bedroom," she said chokily.

The colors swirled again and parted. Meylyne held her breath, expecting to see her mother asleep in her bed but to her surprise the bed was empty, its covers rumpled. Her mother was not sitting at her desk either. Frowning, Meylyne went through all the rooms in her cave and found no sign of her mother anywhere.

She must be out looking for my father. Or for me!

"Show me those garlysle friends of yours!" Blue urged.

At the thought of Trin and Train, Meylyne forgot all about her mother. She longed to see them too.

"Trin and Train's cave," she whispered. "Their bedroom."

Blue edged closer to the diamond. As the colors swirled and faded away, Meylyne's heart gave a jump. Instead of being in their nests, asleep, the twins were up and whispering by candlelight.

"Awesome—they're awake!" Blue murmured. "Can you turn up the volume? I want to hear what they're saying!"

"Forte," Meylyne muttered.

The twins' whispering was suddenly amplified. Train, sitting on the right, was in mid-sentence.

". . . can't believe they took her to the Shadow Cellars," she said. Her voice sounded tinny and small.

"I know—I overheard Father say that Groq won't stand for it," Trin replied. "She is his family after all."

Meylyne's stomach tightened. They were talking about her mother.

"Won't stand for it? What do you mean—you think he'll go to war?" Train asked.

"How would the Above-Worldians find time to fight *us?* They're too busy fighting each other! You know the Welkans were rioting at the castle gates yesterday," Trin replied.

The twins jumped as another voice boomed from outside.

"Trin, Train, are you still up?"

At the sound of their father's voice, the twins snuffed out the candle and crawled into their nests. The diamond became quiet and dark aside from a glow around the outside. With shaking fingers, Meylyne waved her hand over it and the glow subsided.

"My mother is in the Shadow Cellars," she murmured.

For a moment, no one said a word. Hope and Grimorex looked as shocked as Meylyne while Blue's eyes darted from Hope to Grimorex to Meylyne in the hope that someone would tell him what that meant.

Meylyne felt numb inside.

It's because of you, a voice whispered in her head. As if reading her mind, Hope nuzzled her shoulder with his nose and said, "Not your fault."

"Absolutely," Grimorex agreed in a low voice. "This sounds like sphers' work to me. More must have escaped than we thought. They're turning everyone against each other."

From the middle of the lake, a marsh bird wheeled out from the water, shimmering drops falling from it as it flapped overhead. Meylyne watched it fly away with unseeing eyes. One thing was certain now.

Mother can't help us fix this.

"Okay," she said at last. "Tell me more about this eagle."

13

The Palace of Lions

MEYLYNE WOKE UP EARLY THE NEXT MORNING WITH A pounding headache. She had spent a restless night, dreaming of shifting sands that crumbled beneath her and a door in the distance that she needed to reach but the sands kept moving it further away.

Pulling aside the curtain, she peered outside. It was still dark except from a layer of gold blanketing the ground in the distance. The sun would soon be up. Slipping her feet out from under the blankets, she slid out of bed and padded down the hall, down the stairs and into the kitchen. Grimorex was already up, chatting with some fairies while a pot bubbled on the stove. He stopped talking when he saw her.

"Good morning," he said. "Did you manage to sleep?"

Forcing herself to smile, Meylyne nodded.

Grimorex eyed her. "You look dreadful. Here," he dragged over a low, heavy armchair in front of the fireplace. "You sit here and I shall bring you a cup of chocolate."

Meylyne climbed into the enormous armchair and held out her hands in front of the fire, crackling in the fireplace. After learning that Glendoch was on the brink of civil war, they had come back to the castle. Whatever else Grimorex was going to show them could wait—he said they had to be up early if they were to get to the Palace of Lions by dusk. He was quite sure that the lions would know where to find the eagle, no matter how well hidden he was.

Footsteps approaching shook Meylyne from her thoughts. She looked up as Blue walked into the room. His hair stood on end and he had dark shadows under his eyes. Clearly he had not slept well either.

"Morning," he said, attempting to be cheerful. Two fairies brought him a donut and he sat before the fire, munching on it.

Meylyne felt a pang of pity for him. With her mother imprisoned, there was no one that could restore his memory or his size. He was probably as scared as she was.

"Good morning," Meylyne replied. "When are we setting off?"

"Just as soon as I get dressed," Grimorex said. "Which I shall do right now, if you'll excuse me." He laid two plates piled high with donuts and fruit on the floor next to Blue. Please help yourselves."

Meylyne slid off the chair and sat next to Blue. Reaching for a cinnamon donut with white sprinkles, she nibbled on it and slid him a sidelong glance. He was deep in thought. She'd never seen him so serious before.

"You know Meylyne, we may not be the only ones after that feather."

The donut in her mouth suddenly tasted like clay. She swallowed it with difficulty.

"What?"

"Yeah. I bet Queen Emery's after it too. Think about it. She imprisoned your mother—Glendoch's most powerful sorceress. With that eagle's feather, who could stop her?"

Before Meylyne could reply, the door opened and in padded Hope. He had spent the night outside and his coat gleamed with dew. He wasted no time in coming to the point.

"Been thinking. Maybe others after feather too. Better I stay here while you go Palace of Lions. Watch more in Diamond Chariot. Find clues."

"No! I want you to come with us!" Meylyne exclaimed.

"Hope is right," Blue argued. "We were just saying the same thing about others wanting the feather too. I bet if Hope studied the Glendoch Castle, he'd find some answers!"

"But the Palace of Lions sounds scary—I want Hope with us. He knows lions better than we do!"

"Actually I know the lions best of all," Grimorex boomed as he strolled into the room. He looked very different. Gone were the satin clothes and thigh-high boots and in their place a simple gray suit. "I grew up there. And there's no danger to be had at the Palace of Lions."

Meylyne eyed him.

"No danger? Then why are you dressed like that?"

"One just never knows with Queen Scarlet. She is the Lion Queen and she is subject to moods. She detests finery." He gave Meylyne and Blue a sweeping glance. "She'll have no problem with you two, that's for sure."

Slinging a hat around his neck, he strapped a pouch to his chest.

"Are you ready to go?"

Meylyne dropped her uneaten donut back onto the plate.

She did not feel ready. So much felt wrong about what they were about to do. Not wrong exactly, but not right either.

"Something's bothering me. If this eagle exists, how come I've never heard of it? I mean, I know we don't hear much about stuff outside of Glendoch, but something with Trisdyan's powers? I'm sure we'd have heard of *that!*"

"Bet royals *do* know of it," Hope cut in, "but they fear alchemy. Do much to suppress knowledge of it."

"Agreed. I'd wager my life that Glendoch's royals are sitting on bigger secrets than this," Grimorex replied darkly.

"Exactly! That why I want watch Diamond Chariot—see if can find more secrets," Hope said. "Lions no dangerous Meylyne—we have treaty, remember?"

Meylyne scowled. She desperately wanted Hope with them, even if what he said was true.

"What makes you so sure the lions will know where this eagle is if it's such a secret?" she asked Grimorex.

"Oh the secret is safe with them. Lions and eagles are kindred spirits—both value freedom above all else. They care nothing for the burden of power," Grimorex explained. "Now if you've quite finished with all the questions, it's time to go!"

Grimorex picked Meylyne up and stuffed her into his pouch. He tried to do the same with Blue, but Blue immediately scrambled out and climbed up onto Grimorex's shoulder.

"Suit yourself but we'll be moving quickly so you'd better hold tightly!" He glanced down at Meylyne. "Is that settled then? Hope will stay here while we go to the Palace of Lions?"

Meylyne sighed. Deep down she knew it made sense.

"I suppose so."

"Excellent."

Strolling outside, Grimorex called over his shoulder, "Bye Hope! If you need anything, just ask one of the fairies. They know how to operate the Diamond Chariot too. We'll see you in two days!"

Meylyne was dangerously close to tears as they strode off. She felt dejected and bone-achingly tired. Up above, she heard Blue telling Grimorex about how he had come here. His voice faded to a drone as she got lost in her thoughts so she was startled when Grimorex warned, "Don't eat those. They're poisonous."

Meylyne popped her head up. Grimorex's loping strides had already brought them deep into his forest to a thicket bursting with thorns and bright red berries.

Blue chucked the berry away.

"I have a question. If it's so hard for Queen Emery to rule Glendoch all by herself, why doesn't she just appoint the Rose House another monarch?"

"She can't just appoint someone else—the Roses would have to agree on someone and they can't seem to do that. They fight about it all the time," Meylyne replied, yawning.

"Not to mention that the Roses have had bad luck with that role," Grimorex added. "Princess Amber had an older sister who died at birth, you see, so deep down, the Roses fear the role is cursed. Long ago, the Rose line was magical but they forsook their alchemical roots. There are some that believe they are being punished for that."

Meylyne mulled this over as the scenery continued to whiz by. Before long they reached the outskirts of the forest, emerging to find themselves at the edge of an enormous crater, strewn with Spanish Feather-Coils, some standing, some felled. Grimorex crossed it in two steps, and then wound his way through a valley littered with glittering black boulders.

Around noon they stopped for a quick lunch of crusty rolls, cheese and peaches. It started to rain—a warm, soft rain that smelled like pine. Grimorex put on his hat, underneath which Meylyne and Blue stayed perfectly dry. As they set out again, the black boulders shrank down to pebbles and slowly petered out, leaving nothing but rolling hills on either side. Eventually Meylyne was lulled to sleep by the pitter-patter of raindrops above her head.

It was just approaching twilight when she awoke. Now they were near the edge of a cliff, carpeted in tiny blue flowers. The rain had stopped, leaving the air fresh and clean.

"Almost there!" Grimorex announced. "This cliff overlooks the Lions' Palace. I can't wait for you to see it."

Within five minutes they had reached the cliff edge. Grimorex knelt amidst the blue flowers and they all peered down below.

"Wow," Meylyne breathed. "So *that's* the Palace of Lions."

Slabs of jade spiraled out of the ground, glowing softly in the setting sun. From above, it looked like a labyrinth. Some slabs were upright, others were on their side and some rested at diagonals upon each other. Trees and plants of all shapes and sizes grew throughout the palace, including a sprawling leafy plant with violet blooms that lined the floor like a purple and green carpet.

"It's really cool!" Blue said.

"Yes it is. The tusked lions are quite well-known for their prowess in architecture and building. Now. When the lions see us coming, they will send two sentinels to ascertain our intentions. Please let me do all the talking and say nothing unless directly addressed," Grimorex said.

Meylyne and Blue nodded. They were perfectly happy to do as little talking as possible.

Grimorex began the steep descent down a path that was so narrow he had to side-step. They had almost made it to the bottom when he stumbled on a loose boulder and slid clumsily down the last twenty feet. The boulder landed on his toe, causing him to hop up and down, swearing, while Meylyne and Blue bounced around like rag dolls. Meylyne thought she she saw something fly past her nose but she forgot about it almost immediately as two golden lions emerged from the dusk, their tusks gleaming silver in the dimming light. One of them threw back his head and roared.

"Please speak in English, brother," Grimorex requested, instantly ignoring his toe. "Regrettably, my two friends here do not understand your tongue."

The lion narrowed his eyes. "Why do you call me brother?" he growled.

"Because I used to live here many years ago and consider all tusked lions my brothers. You must be quite young not to know me!"

The second lion came forward. He was smaller than the other. "I know you, although I was a cub when you were here. That was a long time ago, Grimorex. What brings you back?"

"I come to pay a visit to my old friend, Queen Scarlet and to offer her a gift."

Meylyne gave Grimorex a sharp look. *What gift?*

"A gift?" the lion growled.

"Indeed, a gift, and please forgive me for keeping its details a secret, for I wish it to be a surprise for the queen. Would you be so kind as to escort us to her?"

"Who are your friends?"

"Meylyne and Blue. They are on a quest and require the queen's considerable knowledge if they are to succeed."

Apparently satisfied with all this, the lions nodded and stalked off toward the castle.

"Now we must follow at exactly five paces behind them," Grimorex explained in a low tone. "You see the lions are a noble breed. It would never do to say, 'we are here to ask the queen for something and have a gift for her in return.' Everything must seem to be bestowed as a favor and anyone who breaches this basic rule gets eaten."

"What gift did you bring?" Meylyne whispered.

"I didn't. We left so hastily that I forgot all about it but not to worry. I'll figure something out. Now be quiet. Whispering is considered bad manners."

Meylyne felt a bead of sweat trickle down her forehead as they followed the lions through two pillars into the palace. She vowed not to speak at all if possible.

"Wait here," the bigger lion growled before both lions disappeared through a thick curtain of violet and green vines hanging from an arch.

Meylyne and Blue looked around. The jade slabs were far bigger than they had looked from up on the cliff. They spiraled up and around them with lots of passageways leading this way and that.

"Easy to get lost in here," Blue whispered.

"Shhh!" Meylyne wiped her clammy hands on her tunic,

which, she noticed in dismay, was smeared with dirt and full of wrinkles. "No whispering!" She turned to Grimorex and, in a low voice that she hoped would not be counted as whispering, said, "Have you thought of a gift for the queen?"

"Yes. No time to explain but just go with it. The most important thing you can both remember now is not to show fear. It makes the lions hungry . . ." He broke off, his eyes fixed on a spot behind Meylyne, saying,

"Queen Scarlet!"

Whirling around, Meylyne held her breath as the queen of the tusked lions padded into the room. She wore no crown on her head but there was no doubting that she was the queen. Although flecked with gray, her fur was the color of finely-spun gold and her eyes looked like two suns setting. At the end of each tusk a single diamond shone.

Grimorex knelt at the lion queen's paws, beaming from ear to ear.

"Thank you *so* much for receiving us on such short notice. Words cannot begin to describe how *lovely* it is to see you again."

Queen Scarlet regarded him as he kissed her front paws.

"It is a pleasure to see you also Grimorex, although it has been too long." Her tone held a hint of steel. "Please, be seated. Would you like something to drink?"

"That would be wonderful, thank you," replied Grimorex, motioning to Meylyne and Blue to sit on the floor.

A sleek, silver lion with a white mane trotted in. On his head, he carried a large shell full of a sparkling liquid. Grimorex took this and the lion moved soundlessly to the vine curtain where he sat, watching.

"Thank you, Corkk." Queen Scarlet turned back to Grimorex. "Who are your friends?"

"Ah yes. This is Meylyne of Glendoch and that is Blue of . . . we're not quite sure where."

Queen Scarlet bowed her head at each of them, her gaze lingering on Meylyne and then she turned back to Grimorex with an expectant air. He smiled at her.

"You're probably wondering what brings us here but first, please let us offer you a gift."

Queen Scarlet stifled a yawn. When Grimorex did not say anything else, she added impatiently, "Of course. Offer away."

Grimorex took a sip of the water and then handed the bowl to Meylyne. He gave her an odd smile and a warning bell went off in her head. From the look in his face, it was almost as if he intended to make a gift of her!

"Enough with the theatrics, Grimorex! What is this gift of yours? I wish to get on with things!" Queen Scarlet ordered.

"Well," Grimorex replied, dabbing his mouth. "That, your Grace is your choice. Meylyne here is an alchemist and can conjure up anything you desire!"

14

The Bargain

MEYLYNE'S INSIDES TURNED TO ICE AND SHE GAPED AT Grimorex. What was he playing at? Part of her wanted to snort with laughter but she was painfully aware that the queen was staring at her. Blood rushed to her face making her skin prickle as she forced herself to smile.

"*You* are an alchemist?" Queen Scarlet growled, her eyes narrowed.

Not trusting herself to speak, Meylyne just nodded. *But not a very good one,* she wanted to add.

There was a pause while Queen Scarlet regarded her. Now she seemed anything but bored.

"You must forgive me if I seem surprised. Long have I wanted to meet someone from our frozen neighbor to the east—shrouded in secrecy as you are—and now I find myself in the presence of one of its alchemists, no less. I thought your sort had all died, but one."

"No, not quite," Meylyne murmured, blushing.

"Not quite," Queen Scarlet echoed. "And are you fully fledged or still an apprentice?"

"Oh I'm—"

"Of course she is fully fledged!" Grimorex interrupted.

"Trust me—I would never bring an *amateur* into your home."

Meylyne cringed. Amateur was the perfect description for her. This was going from bad to worse.

"I do trust you Grimorex, although you suffer from misplaced optimism at times."

Queen Scarlet rose to her feet and stretched. Strolling over to Corkk, she exchanged a few words and then returned to the center of the room.

"You must forgive my bluntness but I need to ask what it is you want in return for such a gift. This sort of generosity rarely comes without strings attached."

Grimorex blinked. He had clearly not been expecting this. Meylyne guessed it was a huge breach of the lions' code to ask such a thing. An uncomfortable silence settled upon the room as Queen Scarlet waited for him to answer. When he remained quiet, her gaze shifted to Meylyne, and then Blue.

"We need a feather from the oldest eagle alive—the one descended from Trisdyan. Grimorex said you'd know where he was. Do you?" Blue asked.

He obviously felt no need to ask forgiveness for *his* bluntness. Meylyne held her breath, wondering what the queen would say. Part of her was scared but another part was relieved to have everything out in the open.

"I see." Queen Scarlet did not seem surprised by the question. She gave Meylyne a calculated look. "You must be a mighty sorceress indeed if you believe you can handle an instrument of such power."

Meylyne groaned inwardly. Not *everything* was out in the open yet.

"Oh she is!" Grimorex said brightly. "You must excuse her modesty. As you know, in Glendoch's New Order, the alchemical profession is no longer held in high esteem. She has learned to downplay her talents."

"Hmmmm." Queen Scarlet exchanged a look with Corkk. "Well in that case I thank you for your offer and gladly accept your gift now that I know the terms that come with it. Please, follow me."

Rising to her feet, Queen Scarlet padded from the room with Corkk at her heels. As soon as she was no longer in sight, Meylyne turned to Grimorex and mouthed, *This was your plan? I can't do this!*

You'll be fine, Grimorex mouthed back. *Go!*

Meylyne looked to Blue for support but he just grinned and gave her a thumbs-up. Fighting the urge to turn them both into toads, Meylyne followed the lions up some steps to a stone balcony. She would never pull this off—never. She would mess up the incantation, like always, and then the lions would eat her. Perhaps she could complain of a headache—say she had to do it later. Then they could escape in the night—

"For my gift, I would like a ceiling to protect us from the rain."

Meylyne's thoughts screeched to a halt. Looking around, she realized they had climbed to the top of the palace. Night was falling, filling the sky with stars and the palace jade glowed ghostly green in the moonlight.

A ceiling wasn't actually all that hard. A one-part incantation if she remembered correctly.

"And it needs to be invisible."

"Pardon?" Meylyne stared at the queen. "*Why?*"

Apparently that was wrong thing to say. Meylyne shrank back as the queen's eyes hardened; the sunsets within them flaming into fire.

"I'm not saying that's a problem!" she added quickly. "I've just never seen an invisible ceiling before. Why would you want that?"

"I see no reason why I should explain myself but if you must know it is because nothing can interfere with the natural beauty of our palace. I wish to see the stars above me as I sleep at night but no longer do I wish for the rain to seep into my crumbling bones. Does that help?"

The queen's icy tone did anything but help. Reddening, Meylyne nodded.

"Of course. I'm just a bit rusty on my invisiblizing incantation. I'll just, um, find it in my book."

Turning her back on the queen, Meylyne shook her book out of her rucksack. She didn't want her to see how badly she was shaking as she flipped through the pages.

"There we are—an incantation to make something appear as though it isn't there at all," she said, trying to sound like it was no big deal as she skimmed over the spell.

Oh no. It's three parts and that middle part makes no sense at all.

"Delightful. Shall we get started then?" Queen Scarlet asked.

Meylyne licked her lips. If she said no, they would all suffer for it. If she said yes and failed, they would suffer for it just the same. But if she said yes and succeeded—

"Sure."

As soon as the word was out of her mouth she knew

she'd made a mistake. Her hands were icy-cold and trembling like two leaves in a storm. She shook herself.

Just focus Meylyne. And follow the book to a T—that's what Mother would say.

Flipping back through the pages, she found the first incantation—the bit to create the ceiling. This part really didn't look that hard. Fixing her attention on the top of the palace, she cleared her mind and began to mutter the words to the spell. Before long, a wisp of smoke materialized before her eyes. Then another, and another, and then *hundreds* of wisps of smoke were curling around one another like wool on a loom. They spread across the top of the palace, reminding her of the tide coming in. Seconds later, a gray roof sat atop the palace walls.

A thrill surged through Meylyne. *It worked!*

"It's not exactly *invisible,*" Grimorex remarked.

Meylyne scowled at him. She still had half a mind to turn him into a toad.

"That's just step one. *Now* I'll make it invisible."

Out of the corner of her eye she saw Blue grinning. He probably thought she had it in the bag but what he didn't know was that this bit was *much* trickier—a three-part incantation, no less. She turned to the spell and read through it again.

Part two really doesn't make any sense. It doesn't look like it belongs at all.

A bead of sweat trickled down her face as Queen Scarlet gave an impatient cough behind her. She would just do the spell as it was in the book. That's what her mother would tell her to do.

Clearing her throat, she raised her palms and began to chant the spell, trying to keep the words from tripping over each other as her fingers stabbed the air. A three-part incantation meant she had to weave three meanings into each word that she uttered. It required the utmost concentration. The air tingled as the incantation began to work.

". . . eeska loosita numevo *ma!*"

The spell was done.

Meylyne held her breath, her eyes glued on the roof above as it dissolved into tiny dirt-like particles. It was working! Any minute the grains of dirt would blow away.

Wait a minute. The particles aren't blowing away. It looks like they're re-forming into something.

Blue tugged on her sleeve. "Meylyne—are those . . . ?"

His words were swallowed up as an intolerable noise filled the air. A medley of croaking and belching was the only way to describe it. The star-crusted sky was gone. In its place, a mottled green mass writhed.

"Toads?" roared Queen Scarlet. "You've made me a ceiling of toads? Is this your idea of a joke?"

"No, it's not a joke! It's just a mistake—I'll fix it!" Meylyne cried.

"A *mistake?*" Queen Scarlet swatted Meylyne's spell book out of her hands. "How *dare* you wreak havoc on my Queendom this way? Off to the burrow while I decide what shall be done with you!"

Two lions appeared out of nowhere. Growling, they herded Meylyne and Blue toward the steps.

"Wait, please—" Meylyne begged.

One of the lions thrust his massive head into Meylyne's

face and his roar hit her like a hurricane. She fled down the steps with Blue close behind.

"And you," Meylyne heard Queen Scarlet snarl. "What have *you* got to say for yourself?"

Grimorex's reply faded away as they descended down the stairs. They did not stop at the floor from which they had come up; they kept going down, underground. The light faded away and when they reached the bottom of the steps it was almost pitch black.

"Keep walking," a lion growled behind them.

"We can't see anything," Blue protested. "Where are we going?"

"There's a cave around the corner. You'll stay there until the queen has decided how best to make you suffer. Now walk!"

"But we're here to help," Meylyne pleaded as she felt her way along the wall. "And I'm a Glendochian! She can't hurt us—our treaty says so."

The lions chuckled nastily as they continued down the tunnel. With a sinking sensation, Meylyne realized that the lions couldn't care less about the treaty right now.

"In there," the lion growled, gesturing to a cave on the right. It appeared to be empty aside from a torch sputtering on the wall. It also smelled like moldy socks. When Meylyne and Blue hesitated, the lions shoved them with their heads and they fell inside. In a flash, Blue was on his feet and he ran to the cave opening just as a boulder rolled in front of it. He slammed his hand into it in frustration.

"We're good and trapped now!"

The light from the torch was so dim that Meylyne could only see his outline as he turned around to face her.

"Toads—seriously?"

Meylyne sank her head into her hands.

"Oh don't start! I don't know *how* that happened. I was so nervous I must have messed up the incantation somehow."

She didn't dare tell him that she had been thinking about turning Grimorex into a toad just seconds before. That must have been why it happened.

Shaking his head, Blue moved around the edge of the cave, his fingers crawling over the walls.

"Well come on—help me see if there's a way out anywhere."

Meylyne pushed herself to her feet with a groan. "There won't be. All we're likely to find are spiders. Or scorpions," she added with a shiver. Taking the torch from the wall, she searched for any sort of passageway. The walls were damp and in places they oozed green slime.

"No way out," she sighed after she had been around the entire cave. Putting the torch back, she rubbed her arms. "But no nasty bugs either—they hate wet."

Blue stamped his feet. "Can't say I'm a huge fan of it right now either. It's freezing down here!"

"I know—"

Meylyne stopped talking. Something behind Blue had moved. Whatever it was, Blue heard it too and he turned around.

"It's the boulder—it's moving. Someone's trying to get in!" he whispered.

From behind the boulder there came a grunt, then a swear, and then another grunt. With each grunt, the boulder moved a little bit. Drawing his sword, Blue moved in front of

Meylyne. There was one more, big grunt and the boulder fell to the ground with a thud.

Meylyne's hands flew to her mouth when she saw who stood there.

"*You!*" she gasped.

15

An Unexpected Visitor

AN ENORMOUS TUSKED LION STOOD IN THE ENTRANCE. It was the lion from the bridge—the one that had tried to eat them before.

"Don't say another word," he warned. "I'm here to help."

Blue stepped toward the lion, his sword raised high. "Yeah right."

The lion eyed him and his sword. "Oh this is a fine end to my day," he growled. "First I almost dislocate my shoulder on that boulder and now I find myself at the tip of a sword. I'm not going to hurt you, you know. I already told you—I'm here to help!"

In the dim light, Meylyne saw that his eyes had lost the vacant look they had had before. She also saw a nasty scar on his paw from where Blue had slashed him before. Judging by the look on his face, he wouldn't try any funny business again.

"I think he's telling the truth," she whispered to Blue. "Let's hear what he has to say."

Blue glared at the lion. After a second, he lowered his sword. "Go on."

"Why thank you for permitting me to speak in my own

home," the lion muttered. "Your generosity overwhelms me. I overheard Grimorex tell Queen Scarlet that the Great Oaken Mother has been poisoned and that sphers are escaping."

"Yes that's true!" Meylyne replied.

"I know that's true. Nothing else could overcome my will."

The lion stared at her as if expecting her to say more.

"We came here because Grimorex said Queen Scarlet knows an eagle that can help us fix the Great Oaken Mother," she added.

"That she does, but she'll never release his whereabouts to you now. Not after what you did upstairs," the lion said.

"But that was an accident!"

"Oh good. That makes us feel much better. We'll hand over the eagle right away now that we're know you're just *clumsy.*"

Meylyne clenched her fists. The lion had every right to doubt her. *She* doubted herself most of the time. But she knew that she'd get the spell right if she were given a second chance. She just had to clear her mind properly this time. And she needed her book of incantations back.

"Look, you *said* you were here to help," she replied, thrusting out her chin. "I know your code, you know. You're in our debt for your intention to violate the treaty. But if you get me my spellbook back, we'll be even."

She held her breath as the lion studied her. Part of her couldn't believe she'd just talked back to him that way but he was their only hope.

"Maybe he's scared," Blue suggested. "He *is* a bit on the old side . . ."

"Shut up," the lion snarled. He started to pace before them. "Is it true what Grimorex says?" he asked Meylyne. "That you are Meph's daughter?"

Meylyne froze.

"I take that as a yes." The lion's eyes bored into Meylyne. "It must be hard for you—feeling responsible for your father's desire to divide Glendoch. It will not be easy to get your book, you know. Corkk is guarding it and one does not become Scarlet's Lead Lieutenant easily. But if this is what you want then I shall get it for you. And then we are even, you and I!"

"Fine. And by the way, I'm *not* responsible—"

"Now that I am myself again," the lion interrupted, "and my mind is no longer full of sphers, I find myself wondering why they would have wanted *you* of all people out of the way. You may be Meph's daughter but you seem completely harmless. There must be more here than meets the eye."

Standing up, the lion stretched.

"But that is Glendoch for you—riddled with secrets. All right, I am off. If I am not back before sunrise then all is lost for both of us."

With that, the lion slunk out of the cave. There was more grunting and swearing and then the boulder thudded back into place. Meylyne and Blue were once again alone in the dark, damp cave.

At first neither said a word. Blue peered up at Meylyne and saw that she was frowning.

"Don't worry, he'll get the book," he said.

Meylyne nodded.

"I hope so." Wrapping her cloak around her, she hugged

herself. "Why on Glendoch would Grimorex have told Queen Scarlet about my father?"

Blue shrugged. "I guess—"

"And how does everyone even know so much about Glendoch?" Meylyne continued as if Blue hadn't spoken. "Why do they care? We're a dinky little glacier and we're really far from here!"

"Well—"

"I know, I know—it's obviously part of the whole bigger picture that I know nothing about," Meylyne's voice caught in her throat. "The lion was right—Glendoch *is* riddled with secrets and I'm sick of all of them!"

Meylyne's chin wobbled and a tear rolled down her cheek.

"Look—let's not think about that right now," Blue said hurriedly. "This is a *good* thing, this lion helping us. I mean it's a weird thing too—who knew *he'd* show up again? But let's worry that and all that other stuff later. We can only do one thing at a time. You've got a big spell coming up. Isn't there anything you have to practice to make sure you get it right next time?"

"Not really. I don't have my book, remember? All I can do is practice not thinking anything that could get in the way," Meylyne sniffled.

"So do that! Thinking about nothing is *hard*. Come on, I'll help. I won't say a word!"

Wiping her eyes, Meylyne gave Blue a grateful smile. He was obviously trying to cheer her up. Smiling back at her, he sat down and patted the ground next to him.

"Come on, let's practice thinking nothing together."

Meylyne sat down next to him and the two of them lapsed into silence. She tried her hardest not to think about anything but the thoughts kept creeping back into her mind.

What did *that lion mean about Glendoch being riddled with secrets? That would fit into our idea that Queen Emery was the Thorn Queen. But why would she want to destroy her own Queendom? And why* would *the sphers want me out of the way? We thought it was Blue they were after but what if it really was me?*

Meylyne sighed in frustration. None of it made any sense. Digging her hand into her pocket, she fished out the pewter shield that Trin and Train had given her. The feel of the cold metal in her palm and the thought of her friends soothed her. After a while, she was able to clear her mind and the minutes passed, stretching into hours. The cold, damp air of the cave seeped into their bones, freezing Meylyne and Blue to the core. Despite this, Meylyne had almost dozed off when a sharp jab between her shoulder blades jolted her awake.

"Aah!" she cried, startling Blue. "Where's my rucksack?"

Blue stared at her as she jumped to her feet, peering wildly around the cave.

"The lions must have it. What's wrong?"

"My allergy pills are in there and I need them!"

"Why? Unless you're allergic to dirt, there's nothing in here to worry about!"

Nothing to worry about?

An image flashed into Meylyne's mind of what would happen if she did not get back her pills in time.

"Look, Blue, here's the thing—"

She stopped abruptly as a shadow passed over the cave entrance. Both she and Blue ran to it.

"Is that you Lion? *Please* be you!" Meylyne pleaded.

There was a series of grunts and groans and the boulder slowly toppled over. The lion limped inside with Meylyne's book in his mouth. He dropped it into her hands.

"Yes, it is I, with your tatty black book and it had better be worth the fiasco it took to get it! When I finally got into Corrk's room, there was a snake there, trying to switch it with another book! No sooner had I dispatched the serpent when I got chased by some guards and would have been ripped to pieces had I not found a secret hiding place."

Meylyne clutched the book to her. "Thank you! And what about my bag?"

"Bag? There was no bag in our agreement. Most likely Scarlet has it. I'm sure she will return it once you've fixed the horror above us."

"But —"

"We don't have time for this Meylyne," Blue interrupted. "Fix the toads first, then we'll get your bag."

Meylyne clenched her fists. By that time it would probably be too late. *But what choice do I have?*

"Okay," she muttered, flipping feverishly though the book's pages. "First of all I need a reversing incantation. Pretty sure there's one in Level Seven . . . there!"

She stabbed her finger into her book and then gasped as the jab between her shoulder blades came back.

"What's wrong?" the lion growled.

"Nothing. Everyone move back. I don't know if—"

"Just do it Meylyne!" Blue urged.

Gritting her teeth, Meylyne started chanting the reversing incantation. Her hands began to shake. It was the first time she had ever done one.

For all I know, I could turn the toads into slugs, or something even worse.

She drove the images from her mind and finished the incantation.

"Done," she whispered, looking up.

Aside from the *plop-plop* sound of dripping water, everything was quiet. Meylyne stared at Blue.

"No more croaking—do you think the toads are gone?"

Blue's face creased into a grin.

"Yeah—I do!"

Delight surged through Meylyne and she jumped up, whooping with joy.

"I *knew* I could do it! Told you!" she shot at the lion.

"Well done," he growled, with what could almost be called a smile. "Now we are free of that infernal racket and I am free of my debt."

His ears pricked up as a shout was heard from above.

"I must go. The guards will be here any minute."

That sobered Meylyne up. He was right—now that the toads had gone the guards *would* be there at any minute and she still had to invisiblize the roof. Grabbing her book, she found the page she needed as the lion turned to leave.

"Wait!" she cried. "What's your name?"

"Plut."

Meylyne flung her arms around the lion's neck and mumbled into his mane, "Thank you, Plut."

Plut lingered for a second and when he pulled away Meylyne knew he was pleased, even if he still looked gruff. With a terse nod at her and Blue, he left the cave, grunting as he shoved the boulder back into place.

"Remember—you must not speak of our alliance," he growled from the other side.

Meylyne barely heard him. She was already thinking about what she had to do next.

"Just one more step to go," she said to Blue. "The bit I got wrong before."

"Yeah, but you know why, right?"

Meylyne nodded, skimming over the incantation. Then she frowned.

"Wait a minute. It looks different now."

From down the hall came the murmur of voices.

"Whatever—just hurry up and do the spell!" Blue urged.

Meylyne's heart pounded as she stared at the words on the page. She was *certain* they looked different now. The second part had looked wrong before. Now it made sense.

"They're here!" Blue hissed.

Meylyne cleared her mind. Chanting the incantation, her hands twisted this way and that. There was a thud as the boulder to the cave rolled aside. In the archway stood two lionesses.

"Come," one of them growled. "Our Queen requests your presence."

Meylyne had almost finished the spell. Turning her back on the lionesses, she continued to murmur and gesticulate.

"Now!" the lioness roared.

Meylyne jumped.

"I'm coming!"

"Out—go back the way we came," the lioness snarled.

Blue shot her a questioning look, to which she nodded. She had completed the incantation.

With any luck, we can get what we came for now.

16

Meylyne's Secret

MEYLYNE AND BLUE FOLLOWED THE LIONESSES BACK UP the cold, wet steps. Both of them were shivering. This time they were taken to a different part of the palace, to a chamber very much like the one in which they had first met the queen except that this one had two pillows on the ground and one of the walls had been polished to a high sheen. Meylyne's reflection stared back at her from it. She was the color of puddled milk and the way her clothes hung on her she might as well have been a coat rack.

"Wait here," one of the lionesses instructed before both of them trotted off.

Meylyne sank down onto one of the pillows and snuggled into it. It was much warmer than down below. The strain of the night's debacle caught up with her and she felt perilously close to sleep. Yawning, she peered up at the star-filled sky, curving over their heads.

"I *really* hope that last incantation worked. I can't tell if there's an invisible roof up there, or nothing at all."

"Whatever. *I* just hope Queen Scarlet's not mad at us anymore," Blue muttered, plopping down on the pillow next to Meylyne.

"I am not angry," a low voice rumbled.

Suddenly wide awake, Meylyne jumped to her feet as Queen Scarlet and Corkk emerged from the shadows. Blue jumped up too. Obviously, there was another way in behind them. Queen Scarlet's fur shimmered in the moonlight and her copper eyes blazed as she regarded them.

"You may sit," she said, motioning to the pillows.

Meylyne and Blue did as they were told, both sitting up very straight. Queen Scarlet may have said she wasn't angry, but her tone said otherwise.

"So—did the toads disappear of their own accord, or was that your sorcery?" she asked Meylyne.

"That was my sorcery," Meylyne stammered. The words started spilling out of her. "I am *so* sorry about what happened before! I just got so nervous you know, I'm really *not* a very good sorceress yet despite what Grimorex said—

"Wait a minute—where is Grimorex?" Queen Scarlet interrupted. "Someone fetch him!"

From outside the chamber, Meylyne heard the clicking of claws fade into the distance. Then there was silence. Meylyne peered at the queen, not sure if she should keep talking or wait for Grimorex to arrive. The minutes stretched on and she was about to say something just for the sake of it when, finally, she heard Grimorex's voice. He was booming away as though nothing was wrong. When he reached the chamber, he had to stoop under the doorway to enter it and as he straightened up, his head crashed into something above him.

"Ouch! What's that?"

"My invisible ceiling—it worked!" Meylyne cried.

Jumping up, she flung her arms around Grimorex. She

couldn't remember the last time she was so happy to see someone.

"Jolly good," Grimorex said, rubbing his head. "I knew you could do it! But what's it made of? Invisible *cement?*

"I don't know. It serves you right anyway! Maybe next time you'll—*ow!*"

Arching her back, Meylyne jumped away from Grimorex. She felt as if a huge porcupine had pressed up against her.

"What's wrong?" Grimorex asked.

At first Meylyne didn't know what was wrong. Then it struck her. She hadn't taken her pills.

"Oh no—I *really* need my rucksack!"

Whirling around, Meylyne faced the queen looking even paler than before. "Like, now!"

"Whatever for?" Queen Scarlet asked.

"*Please!* I don't have much time. I'll explain later!"

Looking mightily perplexed and none too pleased, Queen Scarlet nodded at Corkk. He slipped away, reappearing seconds later with Meylyne's bag. She pounced on it, strewing its contents everywhere as she ripped through it.

"They're not here!" She clapped her head. "*That's* what must have fallen out when you slid down the cliff Grimorex! *Owwww!*"

The fiery, jabbing pain grew stronger. Now it felt like a swarm of hornets stinging her back. She ripped off her cloak.

"What's going on Meylyne?" Blue cried.

"It's . . . it's . . ."

The room started to spin. The pain was making her dizzy. Then there was a whooshing sound and a gust of wind propelled Meylyne forward. She fell onto her hands and knees.

"Aaaahhhh," she sighed in relief, closing her eyes.

The pain had completely vanished. Now she felt as light as air.

"Meylyne," she heard Blue say as if from miles away. "What. Are. *Those?*"

Twitching a muscle in her back, Meylyne felt a cool breeze waft over her shoulders.

"What do they look like? They're *wings* of course!"

Silence blanketed the room. As she stood up, she caught sight of her reflection in the polished wall. Two very large wings rose up on either side of her, their iridescent, white-and-ivory feathers dazzling in the moonlight. No longer shrunken and cooped up inside her, they stretched blissfully, grazing against the walls of the chamber.

"But . . . how . . . ?"

As Blue struggled to put his thoughts into words, Meylyne realized that everyone was staring at her in shock. Scowling, she folded her wings up against her back and tried to make them as small as possible.

"I'm a garloch remember—half-garlysle? I was born with wings. You can stop staring now—freak show's over!"

She started to put on her cloak but Blue stopped her.

"Don't do that. Why on *Earth* would you hide them?"

"Because they make it so obvious that I'm a garloch! A human with wings? Ugh!" She shuddered in disgust. "As if I'm not weird enough."

"They're not weird, Meylyne—they're *awesome!*"

As he circled her to get a better look, Blue pointed to a spot on her wings where the bones were crooked.

"What happened here?"

"Oh, mother bound my wings when I was little. She hoped to stunt their growth that way. Didn't work."

"That's atrocious," Queen Scarlet growled, speaking at last.

"I'll say it is!" Blue agreed vehemently.

"No it's not! Mother just wanted me to have a shot at a normal life. That's why she made me the pills."

"But if you were born with wings then you should fly. Anything else is *ab*normal!" Grimorex exclaimed.

Meylyne rolled her eyes.

"No—garlysles don't fly. I wasn't going to draw even more attention to myself by soaring around the place!"

"What about the other garlochs?" Corkk asked, speaking for the first time. His voice was low and silky. "Does none of them fly?"

"None of them has wings. I've been told they just look like ordinary humans—not that I've ever met one. I'm the *only* one born with wings that I know of."

Standing up, Queen Scarlet prowled around her. "Well, well, well. What an extraordinary heritage. You possess the alchemy and the Hearing powers of the Old Glendochian Order—*and* you have wings!"

"I know," Meylyne muttered. "It's a pain."

Queen Scarlet and Corkk exchanged a glance.

"Apparently someone is unaware of the gifts with which she has been bestowed," Corkk murmured.

Meylyne wanted to roll her eyes again but thought better of it. She wasn't exactly off the hook with the lions yet.

"They're not considered gifts in Glendoch, sir. They're unnatural," she said as politely as possible.

"*Unnatural?*" Queen Scarlet spluttered. "Have you no sense

of history, child? Do you have *any* idea what Glendoch used to be like? Glendoch was full of winged creatures before the New Order set in. And they were *glorious.* That the garlysles lost the use of their wings is in itself a catastrophe!"

Meylyne shrank back at the wrath in Queen Scarlet's voice. Fortunately, Grimorex came to the rescue.

"I could not agree with you more, Your Grace, but right now we have a more urgent matter to attend to—perhaps we may return to this discussion later?"

Queen Scarlet glared at Grimorex, still bristling. Meylyne was surprised to see that her eyes looked wet as though she was on the verge of tears.

"You are right," she growled, drawing a deep breath. "Let us move to the matter of the Great Oaken Mother. You seek Anzulla, or more accurately one of his feathers in order to heal her. Is that right?"

"Anzulla is the eagle's name," Grimorex explained to Meylyne. "And yes, that is right."

Queen Scarlet nodded but did not say anything right away.

"You do agree that this is a matter of the utmost importance," Grimorex added.

"I do."

"Then what is troubling you?"

"Many things, when it comes to Glendoch," Queen Scarlet snapped. "In healing the Great Oaken Mother, you treat only a symptom of its disease. Glendoch is riddled with secrets and until you have set right its wrongs, you will never truly heal it."

Meylyne frowned.

Again with the Glendoch is riddled with secrets business. What are they on about?

"Do you disagree?" Queen Scarlet demanded, catching the look on Meylyne's face.

"Oh no—it's just I've heard that before," Meylyne said hurriedly.

The queen's eyes flashed and Meylyne was scared that she was going to start ranting again.

"You refer to your father, no doubt. Well it is the truth. And you, hiding your wings, are proof of that!"

Meylyne blinked. "My father? Actually, I wasn't referring to him. I never refer to him if I can help it. I . . ."

She trailed off, remembering that she wasn't allowed to mention the other lion to which she *had* been referring. Once again, Grimorex came to the rescue.

"As before, I agree with you on this, Your Grace, but regardless we *must* heal the Great Oaken Mother," he said. Leaning forward, he clasped his hands together. "Even if it's just a start, it is a matter of great urgency!"

From outside, Meylyne heard two birds call to one another and she noticed that the sun was rising, turning the sky from black to violet. Queen Scarlet sighed.

"Look, it's not that I do not wish to help you with Anzulla. It's that I can't."

"So you don't know where he is then?" Grimorex said, dismayed.

"I didn't say *that*."

Everyone except for Corkk stared at Queen Scarlet, waiting for her to say more. She seemed to be weighing her words. Instead of speaking, however, she nodded at Corkk.

"Where's he off to?" Blue asked as Corkk stalked away.

"You'll see," Queen Scarlet replied.

A few minutes later Corkk reappeared with an odd and rather pathetic creature. It had an eagle's face but its body was leathery and bare like a bat's. A lived red scar streaked down its back. It stared grumpily around the room with bloodshot eyes.

"Ah, there you are." Queen Scarlet's voice took on a very different tone to the one Meylyne was used to. This one was gentle and soothing as if she was talking to a small child. "I am sorry for waking you but there are some people here that wanted to meet you. Meylyne, Blue, Grimorex, this is Anzulla."

"*That's* Anzulla?"

Meylyne's eyebrows shot to the top of her head.

"He's . . . *bald.*"

17

Glendoch in Peril

THE ODD-LOOKING BIRD DREW HIMSELF UP AND SCOWLED at Meylyne.

"Excellent. Top marks for stating obvious."

Meylyne blinked. She hadn't expected him to speak Glendochian. The tusked lions had once lived in Glendoch, so it made sense that they would know the language, but not an eagle. His voice was harsh and clipped.

"Now, now, Anzulla," Queen Scarlet said, still in that same soothing voice. "Try not to be so grumpy please. These people came here in the hope that you could help them."

The bird fixed Meylyne with a querulous glare. "In what way?"

"Well, I was told that your feathers—"

"Aaaah!!!" The bird screeched. "She send you? No more! *No more!*"

Meylyne gaped at the bird as he flew frenziedly upward, bashing into her invisible ceiling. He fell to the ground in a dazed heap and then hopped over to Queen Scarlet, cowering behind her legs.

"No more feathers," he moaned. "She know that."

Meylyne looked from Queen Scarlet to Grimorex, hoping that one of them would explain.

"There, there," Queen Scarlet said. "They were not sent by her. We have already established that."

"Who is *her?*" Blue interjected, walking toward him for a closer look. "And what did she do to your feathers? Did she steal them?"

Anzulla scowled at Blue. At least Meylyne assumed he was scowling. He made that face so often that it was possible that was just his normal expression.

"Now I see you weren't sent by her. Too addle-pated!"

"Addle-*what?* Who is this *her* you keep going on about?" Blue repeated impatiently.

Anzulla did not answer. He just sat there glowering at everyone in sight. Or looking as he always did. Meylyne still wasn't sure.

"Please explain, Anzulla. They really do need your help," Queen Scarlet said.

Anzulla waddled from her shadow.

"Fine. Although much rather be asleep! Feathers no more. Just dust now."

Dust? Meylyne suddenly found it hard to breathe. This was the worst thing ever.

"Why?"

"Patience! I get there! Strange lady come see me. Like you, inquiring after feathers. I surprise she know of feathers' power—most do not. Did not let her know *I* was eagle she sought. Still, she keep coming back. Say Glendoch in great peril and she need feather to save it."

Meylyne and Blue exchanged a glance.

"What did she look like?" Meylyne asked.

"Can't say. Whenever try recall face, just see blur. All I remember how *regal* she was."

"Regal?" Blue echoed.

"Yes, addle-pate. Possess qualities of royalty."

Meylyne and Blue exchanged another glance.

"As if she were a queen. Then what happened?" Meylyne asked.

"One day woke up to dreadful fright—her! Sitting in nook with me! Before I collect wits, start to tingle all over and *poof!* All feathers turn to ash!"

A shiver went through his body.

"She go berserk. Face get blotchy and greenish and she scream and spit at me. Then give me this—" Anzulla pointed to the scar running down his back. "Sure she mean kill me. She leave after that, with ash from feathers. I come here then—need place to hide."

"How awful," Meylyne murmured, looking more closely at the scar. It looked as though he had been burned.

"How did she do that to you?"

Anzulla shivered again. "With wand."

"A wand?" Meylyne looked surprised. "That makes her sound like an alchemist but hardly any use wands any more. Apart from my mother, I don't know of any."

Anzulla shook his head.

"No, don't believe she alchemist. I usually sense enchanted beings when come upon them." He looked sideways at Meylyne. "Like you. But no get that sense with her." He dropped his voice to a whisper. "I think she use Relic."

"A *Relic?* But . . ."

Meylyne trailed off as she heard a rustle at the doorway.

"Enter," Queen Scarlet commanded.

In padded a young lion with a tray of fruit on his head. Bowing down, the tray slid from his head to the ground without spilling a thing.

"Thank you," Queen Scarlet said. "Please wake the others for their morning prayers."

Bowing his head, the lion slunk from the chamber. For the first time, Meylyne noticed that the sky above had brightened into a golden-pinkish color. It was morning.

"Help yourselves," Queen Scarlet added.

Meylyne and Blue did not need to be told twice. They both dove for the fruit at the same time. Meylyne could not remember the last time she had been so ravenous. She grabbed two bananas and crammed a handful of blueberries in her mouth.

"What's a Relic?" Blue asked, stuffing almost an entire kiwi in his mouth.

"Oo tell 'im," Meylyne said to Grimorex, blueberry juice dribbling out of her mouth.

Grimorex shot her a disdainful look and then turned to Blue.

"Relics are instruments of Glendoch's Old Order; enchanted items—you know, wands, crystals, cloaks, that sort of thing—that grew so powerful that they did not need an alchemist to bring them to life. Any old person could master their sorcery, sometimes with disastrous results."

"They're forbidden now," Meylyne added, ripping the peel off an orange. "They were all destroyed when the New Order came in."

Blue looked dismayed. "Destroyed?"

Grimorex nodded.

"At first, they were simply confiscated but then it became clear that the Relic was the master, not the other way around. Although many of the Relics possessed good spirits, the royals decided they should *all* be burned."

"*All* of them? And no one tried to protect them?" Blue cried.

"I don't know. I guess not. It was a long time ago." Meylyne wiped her mouth, smearing orange juice over her cheek. "Some did survive though. They turn up every now and then and you have to hand them over to the royals if you find them."

Blue stared at her. "So, in other words, it'd be easy for Queen Emery to come by one of these Relics."

The orange in Meylyne's mouth suddenly tasted like sand. She swallowed it with difficulty.

"Queen Emery? Why would you say that?" asked Queen Scarlet.

"The Great Oaken Mother said that the Thorn Queen had poisoned her," Meylyne explained. "We thought perhaps that was Queen Emery, because of how she had to drink a broth of thorns when she got Princess Amber kidnapped. But it doesn't make sense. I mean, why would Queen Emery want Glendoch overrun by sphers?"

"She surely wouldn't," Queen Scarlet agreed.

"But think about it," Grimorex said, stroking his chin. "If she is using a Relic to carry out some diabolical master plan, then those feathers would be the one thing powerful enough to defeat her. Especially in the hands of a powerful sorceress like your mother, Meylyne."

"Yeah—and now Queen Emery's gone and imprisoned Meylyne's mom in those dungeons! She's got to be the Thorn Queen!" Blue cried.

"Wait, wait, wait—not so fast!" squawked Anzulla. "Lady that stole feathers live in Land of Snow. My brother follow her to ice palace there."

"The Land of Snow?" Meylyne echoed. "You're sure?"

Anzulla nodded. "According to spies. She still there."

Silence blanketed the room. Meylyne thought about all she had heard of the Land of Snow. In the far northern reaches of Celadonia, it was said to be the land of eternal winter. Aside from a forest of Cedars, nothing lived there any more. Her mother had gone there often in search of Meph—she believed it was where he hid. An awful idea slid into her mind.

What if Queen Emery and my father are in cahoots?

"Well why didn't you say so earlier?" Blue demanded. "This makes things really easy for us!"

"Why?" Anzulla asked.

"We know where the feathers are! So we go to this ice palace, take back the feather ash from this Thorn Queen-slash-Queen Emery, you magic it back into feathers and cure the Tree Mother!"

"Oh is that all?" Meylyne replied dryly.

"Yup, and while we're at it, we'll grab that Relic thing of Queen Emery's and she'll have no more power!"

"She'll still be the queen of Glendoch!"

Blue shrugged and bit into an apple. "You have a better plan?"

Meylyne sighed. She did not have a better plan. In fact, she had no plan at all. Chewing her cheek, she turned to Grimorex.

"What do you think?"

Grimorex was silent for a minute. Then he said, "We came here looking for the feathers and now we know where they are. And we certainly can't leave them in *her* hands, so, yes, I agree—it is worth a try. If we take the diamond chariot we'll get there in a day."

"Yeah—now you're talking!" Blue cried.

Wishing she shared his confidence, Meylyne felt a tap on her shoulder. She turned around to see Corkk looking pained about something.

"I'm afraid I have bad news for you about your book. An intruder entered the castle and stole it. I am truly, truly sorry."

For a split second Meylyne did nothing. She hated to lie to the lions but she couldn't give Plut away. Her hands flew to her face.

"Stole my Book of Incantations? Oh no! What am I going to do?"

She gave Blue a pointed stare as if to say, *help me out of this!*

"Er, do magic without it? It's not like it was all that helpful to you."

Meylyne glowered at him.

"Do not worry," Grimorex interjected. "Your Book of Incantations is bound to you. It will find its way back to you."

"Yes! Of course! I mean—" Meylyne feigned a long-suffering sigh. "I suppose that will have to do. Not to worry then."

Corkk bowed his head but not before Meylyne saw a flash of steel in his eyes. He wasn't fooled, but she had no time to think about that now.

"We have to leave. Thank you, Queen Scarlet, for the lovely breakfast and, well, for not eating us when I messed up my incantation. And thank you, Anzulla, for trusting us with your feathers' whereabouts. I promise we'll return them to you once we've finished with them."

"We see." Anzulla sounded as grumpy as usual but for once he did not seem to scowl.

"It is we that should thank you, for what you are undertaking," Queen Scarlet said, padding toward the doorway.

Meylyne, Blue, and Grimorex followed her out of the palace. Once outside, Queen Scarlet sniffed the air. There was a faint smell of roses. In the distance Meylyne saw the cliff with a bit ripped away at the bottom from where Grimorex had fallen. She supposed she would find her pills there if she looked. Not that she would bother. She liked the feeling of her wings hanging down her back. She turned around to find Queen Scarlet staring at her.

"You know child, many worlds will fall if Glendoch falls," she said.

Meylyne frowned but before she could ask what she meant, Grimorex interrupted. "Yes, well, we must be going! No time like the present for saving a world from falling—that's what I always say!"

Bowing low to the ground, he kissed Queen Scarlet's paws. She regarded him with a twinkle in her eye.

"Still not a fan of farewells, eh Grimorex? Do not let so much time pass before the next time we see you. I still see you as my kin and expect the same respect from you as I do from them. May good fortune be with you all."

Meylyne felt a surge of warmth for the old queen. To

think that all this time the royals had made out that the tusked lions were to be feared when in fact it seemed the royals were the ones to be feared.

"When we're finished with all this, I shall see to it that the tusked lions are invited to visit Glendoch whenever they like!" she said.

"Thank you, child, although we need no invitation to return to our old home. We shall come back when the time is right, believe me."

"I do believe you," Meylyne replied. "Then again, I'd probably believe anything you told me right now. I'm starting to think *anything* is possible."

18

The Land of Snow

THE DIAMOND CHARIOT FLEW STEADILY TOWARD THE Land of Snow. Meylyne, Blue, and Grimorex had wasted no time in returning to Grimorex's castle, picking up Hope and setting off. Hope had seemed quieter than normal. He had said he'd found nothing of interest in the diamond chariot but Meylyne did not believe him nor did she press him. She was too tired for one thing, and she knew he would talk when he was ready.

They had set off at dusk. Curled up in one of the chariot's alcoves, Meylyne poured over her alchemy book. It was so much easier to read now. All the alchemical elements made sense at last—no longer did she feel like she was wading through a mystifying foreign language.

I guess all I did need was practice after all—Hope was right!

As she read through an incantation to change an object's form into something else, one line in particular caught her attention—

In a pinch, rely on your bonds.

They must be talking about her bonds with nature. She read a little further and then, lulled by the heat pulsing through the chariot floor, she fell into a doze. Every time she woke up she read more of her book while above her the sky filled up with stars.

When the sky's edges became tinged with pink, Meylyne crawled out of the alcove, gasping as the cold hit her. It bit into her like nothing she had ever felt before and she wrapped her cloak tightly around her, pulling her hood around her face until only her eyes showed. Her eyes began to stream and she blinked furiously, fearing they would ice over.

Walking to the side of the chariot, she peered out at snow-capped cedars, silhouetted in the distance ahead.

"Cold, isn't it?" Grimorex said, making her jump. She hadn't noticed him join her. He was wrapped in a thick woolen blanket.

"Here, put these on. Glendoch may be a glacier but I guarantee you've never known cold like the Land of Snow before."

He held out a woolen coat, hat, mittens, goggles, and boots. Somehow, they were almost exactly the right size.

"Thanks, Grimorex!" Meylyne mumbled, her lips already numb with cold. "You think of everything!"

A moment later, Blue and Hope joined them. Hope snorted, stamping his feet and steam blowing out of his nose.

"M-morning," Blue stammered, his teeth chattering. "How 'b-bout some breakfast?"

"Put these on first," Grimorex ordered, handing him the same assortment of clothes that he'd given Meylyne. Blue pulled them over his clothes as quickly as possible.

"Thanks!"

Nodding, Grimorex disappeared and fished out some warm croissants and jam from a compartment in the front of the chariot. For a few minutes, everyone munched on them in silence, each thinking about what lay ahead. Blue spoke first.

"So what's the plan? My two cents is that you use your invisibility spell to make us all invisible, Meylyne. That way we can go get the dust and the Relic without being seen."

Meylyne shook her head.

"I thought about that but I'm not one hundred percent sure that I can un-invisiblize everyone afterward! Probably best if I just invisiblize myself and I'll go get the feather dust and Relic on my own."

Blue stared at her.

"You seriously think we'd let you go by yourself?"

"Look, it's bad enough that I've made you half your normal size without making you disappear as well!" Meylyne retorted.

Blue opened his mouth to protest but Grimorex cut him off.

"Let us not argue about this," he said. "As much as I don't like it, I actually think Meylyne is right. I for one am too tall to enter the ice palace without drawing attention to us all. If things turn ugly, each of us could get in the way. Meylyne might end up expending all of her energy protecting us instead of procuring the dust and the Relic and that is, after all, the purpose of this mission."

"No," Blue said, folding his arms.

"Listen—you and Hope can come with me through the forest and wait for me outside the palace. I'll send you a signal if anything goes wrong," Meylyne said.

"Yes," Hope interjected before Blue could protest again. "That what we do. Grimorex right—Meylyne better off without us in way. She magical and can fight magic. We can't."

"Of course we can!"

"No," Grimorex countered. "We can't." He cleared his throat. "I know it's hard for you to comprehend our natural laws. Where you're from, there's next to no alchemy left at all."

Blue stared at him.

"What are you talking about? We don't *know* where I'm from."

"Yes, we do—you revealed it at the Palace of Lions."

"I did? How? What did I say?"

"It was when Meylyne had shown her wings and was about to put on her cape. You said, why on *Earth* would you hide your wings?" Grimorex caught Meylyne's eye. "He's from Aardverd, just as I originally suspected!"

Meylyne gasped and a flake of croissant got wedged in her throat. "Wow—Aardverd—home to Glendoch's Original Six," she spluttered.

Blue gave her a blank stare.

"Huh?"

"The original six humans that Trisdyan summoned to save Glendoch from dying. It's a long story. We'll have to tell you later—but at least you know where home is now!"

"But you said all the passages between our worlds were closed up."

Blue directed this to Grimorex.

"They are. And yet, here *you* are."

Blue fell quiet for a second. Then he shook himself.

"Okay, let's shelve this for now." He gave Meylyne a fierce

look. "I guess I'm outnumbered so I'll let you go into the ice palace alone but the minute Grimorex signals any trouble, I'm coming in!"

Meylyne squeezed his hand.

"I'm counting on it!"

Deep down, she was scared stiff to go by herself. Especially seeing as the first time she'd done an invisibility incantation it had gone quite horribly wrong.

"I'd better have another look at that spell," she muttered. "The last thing I need is to turn myself into a toad."

Pulling off her mittens, she huddled in her alcove and found the chapter on how to invisiblize everything from your breath to a fleet of ships. She read it once, frowned, and then read it again.

"This is so weird."

"What is?" Blue asked.

"It's like I said before—this incantation makes perfect sense now. How did I get it so horribly wrong the first time?"

"You needed practice," Hope said. "Like I say all along!"

"And confidence!" Blue added.

Meylyne considered. Maybe they were right. Practice and confidence *were* important with sorcery. Something still seemed odd but she shrugged it off. She didn't have time to worry about it now. Within just a few minutes she had the incantation memorized. Flipping through the pages, she found the reversing chapter and worked out how to un-invisiblize herself when this was all over.

When this was all over.

She bit her lip. She had a hard time envisioning that. What if the Relic sensed her presence and she had to fight?

She needed some all-purpose defensive spell that could protect her from any curse or incantation. Instinctively she felt for the pewter shield in her pocket. Maybe she could enlarge it and fortify it with . . . *What? Who knows what sorcery the Thorn Queen will use?*

The moonlight reflected off the shield and an idea formed in her mind. *What about some sort of mirror charm? If I could work that out, I could just reflect back to the Thorn Queen any spell she tried to set upon me!*

She ran her finger down the table of contents. Nothing at all on mirror charms. Flipping the book to the back, she skimmed through the index. Sometimes things got hidden.

There!

Like a dusty old gem that had got lodged behind a bunch of stuff in the back of a dark shop she found it—a way to alchemically gild an ordinary object to give it mirroring qualities. The purpose was different—it was supposed to be used to tell the person looking in the mirror secrets about him or herself, but there was no reason she couldn't use it her way too!

Resting the little shield on her hand, she wove the incantation into it. Then she blinked. The shield was fusing with her hand! In a panic, she shook it but the little shield wouldn't budge.

"Almost there," Grimorex boomed, making her jump. "See that lake?"

With an exasperated sigh, Meylyne scrambled to her feet. She would deal with it later. Peering down below, she heard a clink as she rested her hands on the chariot's side. She'd have to get used to that for now.

Beneath her was a crystal-clear lake, its water perfectly still. Chunks of ice lay frozen in it like an unfinished jigsaw puzzle.

"That's the entrance to the Land of Snow," Grimorex said. Banging the side of the chariot, he added, "Lower, please."

As the chariot dipped down Meylyne saw a lonely barge idling by the side of the lake. *At least we won't have to worry about company,* she thought, noting the barge's rotting, splintered condition. *That hasn't been used for ages!*

Flying low over the lake, the chariot skidded to a halt on the other side. A sea of snow, deathly silent and sparkling in the early morning sun surrounded them. Not too far off was a forest and in the distance four glass-like turrets gleamed amidst the white-capped treetops.

In one of those turrets, Meylyne would find the Thorn Queen. She drew a deep breath and turned to face her friends.

"Right. Time to make myself invisible."

Scowling, Blue stared down at his toes while Grimorex forced an unconvincing smile on his face.

"Maybe one of us come—" Hope started to say.

"No," Meylyne cut him off. "I *have* to go alone. Now be quiet so I can cast my incantation!"

Waving her arms, Meylyne muttered the words to the spell. Almost immediately she started to feel giddy.

"Meylyne—your head's disappeared!" Blue cried.

Meylyne touched her face with her fingers. As she did so, her hands began to dissolve before her eyes. Within seconds they were gone. Then her arms, her legs . . . *everything* was dissolving in the same way!

"I have to say, that is pretty cool," Blue said.

Even Hope looked impressed. Only Grimorex still looked serious.

"Very good. Now remember, you'll still make footprints and the like so you're not entirely invisible. From what I know of Relics, it will probably be able to sense you if you're in the same room. It won't be able to do anything about it without Queen Emery but it may have found a way to control her thoughts. Never assume you are safe, just because you can't be seen."

"Of course," Meylyne replied, her voice coming from thin air.

"Head toward the turrets. If I see any danger, I will blow on this whistle—it sounds like the call of a marsh bird. That will be the signal for you to come back or, if you're already inside the castle, for Blue and Hope to go in. Here. I've a whistle for you too."

Grimorex's voice was gruff with tension and Meylyne fought back against the hot sting of tears pressing against the back of her eyes. Slipping the whistle inside her pocket, she took Blue's hand in one hand and rested her other on Hope's neck.

"Don't worry—we'll be back before you know it."

She said it more to reassure herself than him. The three friends jumped off the chariot and began padding silently through the snow. It dipped and peaked, making mysterious patterns on the ground, while the trees stood tall against the sky like giant soldiers. Not a creature stirred—no squirrels scurrying up the trees, no birds pecking for worms. A twig cracked and they all jumped, their heads swiveling from side to side. After a moment of complete stillness, they continued to thread their way toward the turrets.

As they drew closer to the castle the turrets disappeared from the treetops, and then something gleamed straight ahead of them. Meylyne's pulse quickened. They were almost there.

"Right. Time for us to stop," Blue said. He squeezed Meylyne's hand. "The minute we hear any trouble, we'll be there, do you understand?"

Meylyne nodded but then realized they couldn't see her. "Yes. Thank you."

Letting go of Blue's hand, she inched forward toward the castle. She would give anything for her friends to come with her. There were only a few trees between her and the castle now. She stayed behind them for as long as she could, aware that her footprints could still be seen in the snow. Then there was just one tree between her and the castle. She hid behind it and peeked around.

The castle loomed up before her, glistening wetly in the morning sunlight. It was like an enormous block of ice with squares cut out for windows. She shuddered to look at it. It didn't even have a front door—just an archway dripping icicles.

Like a mouth with fangs ...

Pushing the thought from her mind, she tiptoed beneath the dripping icicles and stepped into the palace. Countless rooms surrounded her, silent except for the drip-drop of melting ice. She had no idea where to start—the bubbles in the ice made everything a big blur.

I suppose I'll just have to explore, she thought, wishing all the more that Blue and Hope were there with her. They would know exactly where to go.

Moving slowly through the castle, a numbing cold, spread through her limbs. The rooms had a deserted air to them, as if once they had been full of life but not for a very, very long time. She walked through a kitchen with rusty faucets and cracked, copper pots hanging from icy hooks into a magnificent room with a high ceiling and hundreds of books adorning the walls. Picking up one of the books, she grimaced as it fell apart in her hands—its pages soggy and the words washed away.

She walked through an archway into a circular lobby, in front of which was a curved staircase. Meylyne licked her lips. She knew she would find Queen Emery in one of the rooms upstairs. She tiptoed across the lobby and grasped the banister. The steps looked as slippery as fish oil. Invisible or not, if she fell down them the game would most certainly be up.

Biting her lip, she gingerly placed her foot on the first step.

Just take your time, she told herself. One by one, she climbed the steps, placing each foot squarely in the middle. After an eternity of climbing, she found herself at the top of the stairs. A long, narrow hallway lined with doors stretched ahead of her. By now her legs felt like two wooden planks. Forcing them to move, she peeped into every room. Each one was completely empty—nowhere to hide a purse of dust.

She rounded the corner and stopped. The room to her right was bigger than the rest, its door ajar. Holding her breath, she peeped through the frosty door. There was a big red mound in the middle of the room. Icy sweat trickled down her back and face as she pushed the door open.

The room was bare aside from a white animal pelt on the floor and a bed in the middle. On the bed, a lady in a long red dress lay sleeping, her back to her. She muttered something and Meylyne froze, barely breathing. Five agonizingly long minutes passed and the figure lay still.

Meylyne moved inside. She was almost to the bed when the lady jerked up, so suddenly she might have been a puppet on a string. Meylyne froze.

Don't move, she told herself, her heart hammering in her chest. *She can't see you.*

Meylyne still could not see the lady's face. Her hair was covered by a white scarf. As she slowly turned around, she lifted her hand. Too late, Meylyne realized she held a wand. A sizzle in the air and Meylyne could not move her arms or legs. It was as if they'd turned to clay. Then her feet felt like tiny bubbles were popping inside them. Looking down, a bolt of horror shot through her. Her feet were materializing! The bubbles spread up through her legs, her stomach, her arms and finally her head. She stood there, exposed and helpless but as she stared at the lady staring back at her, she felt more shock than fear.

When Meylyne finally found her voice, she uttered one word.

19

Shadows and Lies

"MOTHER?!"

The lady sitting on the bed, who was in fact her mother, looked almost as surprised as she did. An uncharacteristic smile spread across her face. She flicked her hand and Meylyne found she could move again.

"Meylyne! I must say I'm impressed. I *never* thought you'd make it this far! Sit down," she added, patting the bed next to her. "There's no need to look so alarmed."

"No need to look so alarmed?" Meylyne echoed. "What are you doing here? I thought you'd been imprisoned in the Shadow Cellars!"

"I said sit."

The temperature in the room seemed to drop a notch. Meylyne plopped onto the cold, hard slab of ice while her mother continued to smile as if meeting like this was the most natural thing in the world.

"Actually, fetch that rug," her mother ordered, nodding at the pelt on the floor.

Meylyne slid off the bed and handed the pelt to her. As her mother stood up, the scarf fell off and her long black hair cascaded over her fur-lined, scarlet dress—the only splash of color in the room. This was the first time Meylyne had ever seen her mother with her hair down. She watched as her mother placed the pelt on the bed, and then sat back down.

"There. Now sit."

Meylyne sat down on top of the rug. Her mother's eyes bore into her like flint.

"So you know about the Shadow Cellars." Her mother held out her hand. "I'd like my crystal back please."

Like one in a trance, Meylyne took her mother's diamond from her rucksack and handed it to her. Her mother placed the diamond on the bed next to her. Never once did the smile leave her face.

"I was not in the Shadow Cellars for long," she answered smoothly. "Groq bargained with Queen Emery on that score. He reminded her that I was the one person that could find her son's cure—and you of course. It was quite inconvenient for you to disappear like that."

The temperature in the room seemed to drop even further, if that was possible. Meylyne struggled to respond. Her brain felt full of fog.

"The Wise Well told me to go to the Valley of Half-Light for Piam's cure. I thought it'd be better for me to go than you!"

Her mother lifted an eyebrow.

"And did you go to the Valley of Half-Light?"

"Yes, well, not at first because we went the wrong way." The words started tumbling out, spilling over one another. "But then we found out that the Thorn Queen poisoned the Great Oaken Mother and because of that sphers were escaping into Glendoch! So Grimorex told us about an eagle whose feathers were supposed to have the power to heal the Great

Oaken Mother, only they turned to ash . . . and the Thorn Queen took them and came here!"

"Grimorex—as in the ogre?" her mother asked sharply.

Meylyne nodded. "Do you know him?"

Meylyne's mother tapped her fingernails against the side of the bed.

"I know of him."

Meylyne stared at her mother, waiting for her to say more. The silence stretched on.

"Mother, what are you doing here?" Meylyne implored. "Please tell me! We thought the Thorn Queen was Queen Emery, but now here *you* are."

Standing up, her mother glided to the window and peered outside.

"I came here for the same reason as you—the feather that would cure Prince Piam."

Meylyne frowned. Her mother wasn't telling the whole story. "And?"

"What do you mean, *and?* That's it—that's why I'm here!"

"You're hiding something."

Turning around, Meylyne's mother shot a startled look at her. Then she laughed.

"Meylyne, I'm *always* hiding something. You've just noticed for the first time. This journey has changed you!"

An uneasy feeling grew inside Meylyne as her mother held her gaze. Her eyes looked different—darker somehow.

"You—*you* aren't the Thorn Queen, are you?" Meylyne whispered.

"Thorn Queen, Rose Queen—it's all the same to me."

At first Meylyne just stared, uncomprehending at her

mother. Then her eyes widened as the truth dawned upon her.

The missing Rose princess.

"No, it's not possible," she whispered. "*You* are Queen Amber of Rose?"

Her mother smoothed out an imaginary wrinkle on her dress and her eyes darkened a little more.

"Amber," she sighed. "Always Amber. Fourteen years missing and still in the forefront of everyone's mind while I remain obscured by shadows and lies."

Meylyne's mother returned to the bed. An icicle above dripped a single drop of water between them. Her mother wiped it away.

"No, Meylyne, I am not *Amber*—" her mother spat the name as if a cockroach had landed in her mouth— "I am the the Rose's firstborn daughter—the one that everyone was so eager to forget."

"What are you talking about? The Rose's first baby died at birth."

Her mother chuckled without mirth.

"Such a convenient lie. I did *not* die at birth. I was kidnapped by the Snake People, as all the royals know! And my parents, on their dear sage, Chifflin's recommendation, refused to pay their ransom. Apparently the price demanded was too high."

Her mother patted Meylyne's hand as Meylyne stared at her in horror.

"Oh it wasn't so bad. After all, I had nothing to which to compare the Beneath-World. And the Snake People are far more intelligent than anyone thinks. They taught me all of Glendoch's history."

She stretched her arms above her head.

"And never once did they let me forget my parents' betrayal."

On the mantelpiece, a white spider spun its web. Round and round it went, its silken thread shimmering against the ice. Meylyne watched it, unseeing, as she tried to absorb everything her mother said.

"But, you always said you were a Cabbage-Windian—sold to the Garlysles by your grandmother—"

". . . for a black opal," her mother finished. "Yes dear, I know the story—*I* made it up, remember?"

"But why not just tell the truth? Once you escaped from the Snake People, you could have just gone to the Above-World and told Queen Emery who you were!"

"Oh I did not *escape* from the Snake People. They were all the family I knew. No, your father got me out. I was traded like a prized gem at a fair. In return I had to live with him in the Between-World."

Meylyne's mother took Meylyne's hands and held her gaze.

"Make no mistake. Your father was a very clever garlysle. It is a pity he had to . . . disappear."

All around Meylyne, the ice patterns in the walls swirled and dripped, making her mind even cloudier than it already was.

"*Disappear.* He hasn't disappeared. He's been terrorizing Glendoch for as long as I can remember!"

A smile played upon her mother's face. "Really? Has he ever been caught?"

At this, Meylyne's head began to throb and she got up off the bed. She needed to think. On the mantelpiece, the spider continued to weave her web, going round and round. As Meylyne approached, she crouched still.

"Don't go near that spider, she's frightfully poisonous. One bite and your heart will freeze," her mother warned.

Meylyne moved away, her mind spinning. *If what mother says is true, then I am a Rose Princess!* She remembered the stories of the Roses once being powerful alchemists.

"I thought the Roses' alchemy had died out," she said.

"It almost had. But the Beneath-World is still steeped in sorcery, albeit the dark sort. My powers reawakened there—not completely by any means. But then you were born fully gifted—that was obvious from quite a young age."

Meylyne stared at her mother. "Me? Please! I could never get any of my incantations right. I was the *opposite* of gifted. You were the powerful one!"

Her mother shook her head. "Not without this." She held up her wand. "And you weren't the opposite of gifted. You just never had the right tools."

"I had my Book of Incantations. What other tools was I supposed to have?"

"You didn't really have your Book of Incantations. Not the *authentic* one, anyway. I made sure you never got your hands on that one."

Meylyne stared at her mother. Her Book of Incantations was her source of truth. She had gone through a sacred ritual upon receiving it. It wasn't possible that the one she'd had her whole life was a fake.

But it makes perfect sense, a voice inside her head whispered. *That's why none of your incantations worked. That snake at the Palace of Lions must have switched it for the* right *book, not the other way around!*

"I see you've let your wings grow," her mother said.

Meylyne ignored this.

"No," she said firmly. "I don't believe any of this. You're my mother! You would never lie to me like that for all those years. If what you say is true, then you're an Above-Worldian Queen! Meph," she swallowed, "*disappeared* ages ago. He had no hold over you. Why not just go above ground and tell everyone the truth?"

As Meylyne waited for her to answer she saw something clawing behind her mother's eyes as though trying to get out.

"I'm afraid I'm not that interested in the truth any more. What I want is far simpler—*revenge*."

Meylyne jumped as her mother spat out the word. She did not recognize her any more. Her coldness and reserve had been replaced by fire.

It's just like Grimorex said—the wand has possessed her.

In its corner, the spider continued to spin its web. Meylyne glanced at it and for the first time she noticed something behind the web—a small crimson sack.

The feather dust! I bet it's in there!

Meylyne thought fast. She could stun the spider and grab the sack, but then how would she escape? There was no point in turning herself invisible. The wand could obviously sense her. Besides, she needed the wand too. It was Glendoch's only hope.

And my mother's.

As if she could read her mind, her mother raised her wand. Meylyne dove for the floor as a stream of heat flew over her head. The words from her new incantation book came back to her—

In a pinch, rely on your bonds.

Planting her hands on the floor, she focused her attention on the ice around the bed. The ice creaked and groaned, and then shot up forming a cage around her mother.

For a second, her mother looked as shocked as Meylyne felt.

It worked!

She pointed at the ice above the spider and an icicle fell down, stabbing it. Meylyne winced—she hadn't meant to kill it but there was no time to think about that now. She grabbed the purse from the mantelpiece.

"Put that back," her mother snarled. The ice around her became a waterfall that rushed at Meylyne, who fell to the floor, flinging up her mirrored hand just as her mother shot another incantation at her. The incantation bounced back at her mother, who became as still as a statue.

Must've been another immobilizing charm.

Meylyne knew that the wand was capable of a lot more than that. She wrenched it from her mother at the exact second that her mother un-froze herself. She dashed from the room, aware of a searing heat in her hand and a darkening all around her. Shadows leapt and twisted and her mind clouded with rage.

I can't let the wand get inside my mind!

She had almost reached the stairs when she slipped on the ice. The wand flew out of her hand and bounced to the bottom of the stairs, shattering the ice around it.

This was the worst mistake she could possibly make. Her mother flew past her with uncanny speed and pounced on her wand. Spinning around, she raised it as Meylyne kicked out her feet in front of her. The floor rippled outward, down the stairs, bursting into a wave of ice. It crashed into her mother, sweeping her backward.

"Stop!" her mother thundered, flinging out her wand in front of her.

The wave stood still. One second later and she would have been trapped between it and the wall behind her.

"I really am impressed Meylyne," she said, sliding out from behind the frozen wave. "Where did you learn all of this sorcery?"

Then she hissed, pointing her wand at Meylyne and her spittle turned into a shower of crabs. They scuttled up the stairs toward Meylyne, their tiny pincers snapping before them.

Scrambling to her feet, Meylyne ran into one of the rooms, slamming the door behind her. A few moments later, the crabs scuttled up against the ice, their pincers eating their way through. Meylyne backed away from the door and looked around. The room was empty. It had one window without any glass in it. There was nowhere to hide.

"I'm not going to hurt you, Meylyne," she heard her mother saying, coming closer. "I want you to join me. What is left for you in Glendoch? You will never get back in time. The Great Oaken Mother is about to fall."

At the mention of the Great Oaken Mother, Meylyne felt a jolt of fear. Pushing her hand in her pocket she felt frantically for the dust. It wasn't there. She searched the other pocket.

"Are you looking for this?"

Her mother stood in the doorway, holding the purse. The crabs rushed in around her but with a wave from her wand they all disappeared.

Crouching in the corner, Meylyne fought back tears. She had lost everything.

Think, Meylyne. Just think!

A ray of sunlight splashed through the open window, dividing the space between her and her mother. An idea struck her. She whispered to the sunbeam and it flared up into a stream of bright gold. Shielding her eyes, her mother cried out, temporarily blinded.

Meylyne dashed to the window and climbed up onto the windowsill. It was a dizzying drop to the ground. Flying was her only possible escape but she hadn't flown since she was little! From behind her, her mother said something and the sunbeam burst into flames with a roar. It was now or never. Meylyne leapt. Her wings unfurled. Careening wildly to the left, terror exploded inside her until something automatic in her muscles took over. Her wings pumped and terror melted to exhilaration as she realized the air was holding her up.

I'm flying—I'm actually flying!

Then a fire-bolt punched her left wing. She screamed in pain and the ground came up to meet her fast. Something streaked toward her from the edge of the forest. She landed on her stomach with a sickening thud, all the breath knocked out of her. Eyes closed, she felt the world move beneath her.

"Hold on!" a familiar voice ordered.

Opening her eyes, she almost cried with relief. She had landed on Hope!

Maneuvering herself around, she grabbed onto his mane, dizzy with pain from her wing. He slowed at the edge of the forest and Blue jumped on too. Meylyne steadied him and they both clung on.

Looking back, Meylyne saw two dark shadows speeding behind them, close to the ground. As they drew nearer Meylyne saw eyes pulsing red and dripping fangs. They looked like some sort of demon ghost-wolves. Then they were upon them, tearing at Hope's legs as he ran. Drawing his sword, Blue slashed once, then twice. One creature fell away. The other leapt up at Meylyne, sinking its fangs into her arm and she screamed. Blue slashed again and it, too, fell away.

Muttering under her breath, Meylyne pointed to the trees behind them and their branches leaned to one another like tentacles and grew spikes as they wrapped around each other. Within seconds a thorny barrier was born behind them.

Hope raced on. Now the diamond chariot was in sight, Grimorex peering from its prow. He held open the door at the back and Hope leapt aboard.

The chariot needed no telling what to do. It lifted up and shot off, back to Grimorex's castle. Meylyne, Hope, and Blue plummeted to the back of the chariot. There was a crack and then everything went black.

20

The Snake

THE WET GRASS MOVED LIKE WATER, WHISPERING AT THE gold-tinged air. In the distance was a ring of statues—birds with hawklike heads and trousered legs. Their voices floated to her but she couldn't hear what they said. She tried to run to them … her arm a burning log …

Meylyne sat up, pain like daggers through her right side. She was in the diamond chariot, the wind whooshing above her in the black, star-crusted sky. Grimorex hovered above her.

"Easy! Your head's not bleeding anyway. Just a nasty bump. How's your arm?"

Meylyne noticed that her right arm was bandaged. It felt like it was full of shards of glass. Blue appeared at her side.

"Meylyne! Are you okay?"

Resting her head against the chariot, Meylyne closed her eyes as everything flooded back to her. Something ripped inside her and a weight crushed against her lungs. Next thing she knew she was sobbing—huge wracking sobs that left her shaking and gasping for air.

"There, there," she heard Grimorex murmur as he put his arm around her.

"It's worse than if she was dead," Meylyne wept.

"Who?" Blue asked.

She could not bring herself to answer him. Eventually the tears dried up although the pain remained. She wiped her eyes and for the first time she noticed Hope lying nearby, his legs in bandages. Her stomach lurched.

"Is Hope okay?"

Grimorex nodded. "The wounds on his legs were giving him a lot of pain. I gave him a sleeping potion."

Meylyne rubbed her arm and grimaced. "It's those demon-wolves that my mother sent."

"What?" Blue interrupted. "Your *mother* was there? She helped you fight the Thorn Queen?"

Meylyne faltered as tears threatened to engulf her once again. She choked them back.

"No Blue. The Thorn Queen *is* my mother."

For a moment, no one said a word. Grimorex's eyebrows shot up and Blue just sat there with his mouth wide open. The chariot continued its flight through the night sky. It was a sky Meylyne had seen a thousand times before and yet it looked different. *Everything* looked different. Her world was not the same as before.

"But, but . . ." Blue finally stammered. "*How?*"

Meylyne told them everything. How her mother was the firstborn Rose princess, supposed to have died at birth; how the Snake People had kidnapped her and no one would pay her ransom—

"Wait a minute," Grimorex interrupted. "The *Snake People* kidnapped her? And her parents just *left* her there?" He shook his head, horrified. "What happened to her?"

"She remained their prisoner until—" she took a deep breath. "Are you ready for this? *Meph* got her out. I've no idea why, but I think she killed him for his trouble."

"What? But he's been terrorizing Glendoch—she can't have killed him!" Blue said.

Meylyne shook her head. "*She's* the one that's been terrorizing Glendoch—deliberately pitting the Francescans against the Tyrians. All she wants is revenge." Meylyne looked at Grimorex. "You were right about the Relic possessing her. I managed to get the wand and the feather dust, but then I tripped and lost *everything*."

Meylyne put her hands over her eyes and broke into fresh sobs.

"Why didn't you blow on your whistle?" Blue asked, his face stricken.

"I totally forgot about it." Meylyne took her hands from her eyes. "All that time I spent trying to be so good at sorcery for her—what a joke. Oh, and that's another thing—she switched my Book of Incantations for a fake! That snake at the Palace of Lions must've switched it for the right book!"

Grimorex looked appalled. "She gave you a fake Book of Incantations? But for a fledgling alchemist, that's like . . . oh I don't know . . . denying you a part of your soul! That was to be your source of truth—something gifted to you by the Parliament of Thor-Schael themselves!"

"She obviously didn't care about that. What are we going to do now?" Meylyne looked from Blue to Grimorex. "Deep down I still thought she'd take care of the Thorn Queen. But she *is* the Thorn Queen."

"And *you* are a Rose Royal," Grimorex said softly.

Meylyne began to shake.

"Here." Grimorex handed her a thimble of something. "Drink this. It will help you sleep. And once we get back to my castle, we shall decide what to do."

Decide what to do. Meylyne gulped down the drink. The liquid burned her throat and her thoughts became fuzzy and jumbled. She lay down. *What can we do? The great Oaken Mother is poisoned, Glendoch is on the verge of war and the person behind it all?*

My own mother.

Meylyne awoke the next day to find herself in a large bedroom full of books. At first, she felt disoriented and then everything rushed at her, landing in a jumbled heap in her mind. Through the window next to her she saw a barn and a rose garden. She must be in the back of Grimorex's castle. She could smell the roses all the way from here.

Shivering, she pulled the comforter up to her chin but she still felt cold. She tried to swing her legs out of bed but her whole right sight was numb. Besides she was too tired.

She fell back to sleep.

As the day went on the numbing cold spread through her body. She was secretly glad for this as it lessened the ragged wound left inside her by her mother's betrayal. By nighttime she could barely feel her limbs.

That night Grimorex and Blue stayed by her side, waiting anxiously for some sign that she was getting better. She heard their worried murmurs—talk of poison left behind by her mother's demon ghost-wolves. She stared out the window to the barn where Hope languished, subject to the same sickness as she.

During the night her thoughts sharpened, as if the poison had the opposite effect on her mind that it did on her body. She picked up her incantation book.

"Aethelrix," she announced the next morning. "Those demon ghost-wolves are called the Aethelrix. It takes a Level Eight Enchantment to summon them, and to banish them. My mother probably endowed them with the white spider's poison. That's what's happening to Hope and me. Our hearts are freezing. We won't die. Just hibernate. Forever."

There was no emotion in her voice. She felt nothing as she said it—just a general sense of the effort to speak at all. She lay back down on the pillows.

Out of the corner of her eye she saw Hope and Grimorex exchange a look. Blue thrust her book at her.

"Find the antidote," he ordered. "It's got to be in here somewhere!"

Meylyne took the book and poured through it throughout the day but nowhere in its pages could she find anything that resembled an antidote. The light faded outside as day turned to night. Eventually she fell asleep.

An hour later, she woke up. Something jabbed into her arm. Half asleep, she tried to pull it away but the pain remained. In a ray of moonlight, splashed across her bed she saw a dark smudge. A bolt of terror surged through her.

That's a snake!

Before she could scream the snake locked eyes with her and a fog settled over her mind. Not really sure if she was awake or asleep, she watched as it drew back its head and slithered out of the window. Her arm began to throb and then, like one caught in a net, she felt herself being pulled after the snake.

I must be dreaming, she thought as she climbed out of the window and followed it down the garden path, past the roses and the barn. The pain in her arm grew stronger, spreading through her right side as they approached Grimorex's forest. She had a vague feeling that she did not want to go in there but still her legs pulled her forward and before long the darkness of the forest enveloped her. The snake wound its way down a path that she would have never found, and then it veered off to the left. She followed it through brambles that tugged at her skin and her nightdress, and then her stomach lurched as all of a sudden she was falling—falling or flying, it was hard to tell which—through a tunnel of sparks and a kaleidoscope of color, her hair and nightdress billowing behind her. She landed with a bump, breathless, at the base of a steep embankment.

No, a crater, she corrected herself as she looked around. A crater with white, chalky walls. At the top, it was ringed by trees—silver-willows by the looks of things—their roots snaking down the crater-walls. The moon was a splash of light behind a thin veil of clouds.

The snake was coiled at her feet. Emerald green, it had a pale pink stripe winding around its body and it stared at her with blue eyes that looked oddly familiar.

"Are you all right?" it asked, its voice smooth and silky.

Meylyne blinked. She had not taken it for a Talking Snake. Then she groaned.

"No I am *not* all right."

The pain was spreading was spreading from her arm to her entire body. It made her head throb and her vison blur. A breeze blew bringing with it a hint of roses and a memory struck her—a memory of roses when they had first arrived at Grimorex's. The breeze felt nice and she realized it was hot—too hot—wherever they were.

"Where are we?" she asked. "I want to go back to Grimorex's!"

The snake did not reply straight away. Instead it slithered toward the crater wall. Following it with her gaze, Meylyne frowned. There was something hidden there that she had not seen before—a gate, intricately carved or maybe woven from bleached roots and covered with a strange, undulating pattern.

"Are those—?"

"Scales," the snake finished. "Yes, this is the gate to the Beneath-World."

21

The Beneath-World

"THE BENEATH-WORLD?"

Images of fiery mud and hideous fanged monsters crashed into Meylyne's mind. She tried to scoot away but found she was rooted to the spot.

Then the gate opened, silently receding into the gloom behind it. Heat belched out like a monster's breath. Meylyne struggled frantically as whatever force held her in its power pulled her to her feet.

"No!" she cried. "I can't go in there! Why are you doing this?"

It was no use. She was dragged after the snake as it slithered through the gate, its pink stripe glowing in the gloom.

"Please!" she sobbed. "Stop!"

The force released its hold as the gate closed behind her. Her eyes darting from side to side, she saw she was in a tunnel, its walls covered in mud and full of holes. Every now and then the holes sucked themselves inward and then popped. If not for the snake's stripe glowing ahead of her and a faint effervescence in the mud, the tunnel would have been pitch black.

"Come. You are safe with me," the snake hissed back at her.

Meylyne scrabbled at the wall behind her, trying to find some way out. Mud oozed between her fingers. There was no way out. She looked behind her—the snake was getting further away and darkness was closing in on her. Her breath shortened into ragged gasps as she wrestled with what to do. She was alarmingly short on options.

"You must come—I promise you are safe," the snake hissed.

Meylyne felt the opposite of safe. After a second of agonized indecision, she dashed after the snake. Instantly the walls were alive. The holes in the mud became full of yellow, slitted eyes and forked tongues. The sound of hissing rose up around her.

"What's going on?" she screamed.

"These are the snake people's sentinels that guard the path to the inner Beneath-World," the snake replied. "Don't worry—they won't harm you."

Meylyne choked down a sob, imagining all the snakes pouncing at once, writhing around and sinking their fangs into her. But the sentinels made no move to stop her as she stumbled down the tunnel which grew narrower and hotter with every step. Sweat poured down Meylyne's face and back. Supposedly the mud in the inner Beneath-World boiled with fire.

There was a noise to her right as the mud shifted slurpily and Meylyne whirled around to see a figure emerge from the mud. It was long and sinewy with red gleaming eyes.

"Hello Meylyne, Princess of Rose," the figure hissed in a slow, velvety voice that pronounced her name as "Princessssssss of Rossssssssse."

The figure stepped closer. Now Meylyne saw that its arms and legs were covered in dark green scales and its head more snake than person with its slitted eyes and flat nose. She clapped her hand over her mouth to suppress the scream building inside her. It was a snake person. She was face-to-face with an actual snake person.

The deadliest predator known to Glendochians.

For a second she felt dizzy and the world tilted around her. There was a flash of pink at her side. It was the snake.

"Forget about what you've heard. No one here will hurt you if you do as you're told."

Meylyne kept her eyes riveted on the snake person. It smiled, revealing two curved, glistening fangs.

"Please put this on."

Meylyne backed away as the snake person handed her a bundle.

"Is that a snakeskin?"

"Yes. It will protect you from the fire when we meet with Borghesia."

"Meet with Borghesia? Who's that?" Meylyne's voice was little more than a squeak.

"Borghesia is herself."

Meylyne took the bundle but made no move to put it on.

"Put on the snakeskin," the snake urged. "I promise Borghesia will answer all your questions. She will not harm you."

Meylyne had no choice but to do as she was told. Stepping into the snakeskin, she zipped up the front and pulled the hood over her head. It covered her face entirely, leaving two small holes for her eyes and mouth. The snake person handed her a pair of goggles. A giggle, bordering on hysteria, bubbled up in Meylyne's throat as she pulled them on.

I'll look like a bug-eyed snake.

The goggles were tight and restricted her vision. Sweat poured from her body beneath the tight snakeskin suit, which pressed stickily against her skin.

"I'm going to suffocate," she muttered.

"No you won't. Follow me."

The snake person disappeared back into the mud from which it had emerged. Meylyne stared at it in alarm. No way was she walking in there. An arm snaked out and grabbed her wrist, pulling her forward. A terror unlike any she had ever known before spread through her as she found herself completely enclosed in red, fiery muck. Spots appeared before her eyes.

Calm down, Meylyne. Breathe normally! She forced herself to take deep breaths and as the spots cleared, two things dawned on her simultaneously—she could breathe *and* she could see. Patterns swirled in the glowing mud, displaying an intricate system of levels, hallways, stairs and rooms.

"Come. You will meet with Borghesia through here," said the snake person.

Meylyne followed the snake person up some stairs into a large hallway or maybe a room—it was hard to tell in the eerie glowing light—in which three more snake people waited for them. One—Meylyne guessed it was female—sat on the floor, her legs curved, or rather coiled beneath her. Her scales were a brighter green than the others and some scales seemed tinged with pink. The other two stood on either side.

They look hungry.

As if she could sense Meylyne's terror, the sitting snake

person waved her arms and the other snake people disappeared.

"There," she said in a voice that was half whisper, half hiss. "No need to worry. Please, sit. I am Borghesia."

Meylyne sat on the floor. It felt like sinking into a fur rug.

"Well, well, well," Borghesia said, her eyes glittering. "Princess Meylyne of Rose. Long have I waited to meet you."

"Me?" Meylyne rasped.

She was desperately thirsty. Borghesia uncoiled her legs and stood up, reaching for something that she handed to Meylyne.

Meylyne eyed it suspiciously. It looked like a cup of water. "What is it?"

"A cup of water."

Meylyne took a sip. It tasted like water. She decided to drink just enough to wet her throat but ended up slurping the whole thing in noisy gulps. The drops that fell sizzled into tendrils of steam as they hit the ground.

Borghesia sat patiently, waiting for her to finish. Meylyne flushed, suddenly aware that *she* must seem the barbaric one.

"Thank you," she mumbled. "Why have you been waiting to meet me?"

Borghesia stretched her legs before her.

"I imagine your mother told you half of her sad story. What exactly did she say?"

"That your people kidnapped her when she was a baby," Meylyne whispered. Her voice sounded warbled and she cringed at the hint of accusation in it.

Fortunately, Borghesia did not seem to take offence.

"Well that is certainly true," she said comfortably. "Now allow me to fill you in on some details."

Pulling out something from behind her, she placed it on the ground. Meylyne's eyes widened. It looked just like her mother's crystal.

"Is that *another* piece of the diamond chariot?"

"It is."

Borghesia hissed at the lump of diamond. Colors swirled inside it and pale images flickered to life. Meylyne recognized the building that came into focus.

"That's Glendoch Castle!"

Drawing nearer, she watched as a tall, willowy figure approached, a hood covering its face. When the figure reached the front door, a boy, around Meylyne's age opened it. There was no mistaking his hedge-hoggy face.

"And that's a young Chifflin!"

Chifflin held open the door and the figure followed him into the castle, up a winding staircase into a bedroom on the left. The room was richly furnished with a four-poster bed inside. In it a woman slept. To the side a man poked at a fire, guttering in the grate. He looked up as the willowy figure entered, his eyes wary yet hopeful. The figure bent over the sleeping woman, took hold of her wrist and lifted it to its mouth.

"Oh!" Meylyne gasped. "That stranger just *bit* the lady!"

Inching even closer to the diamond, she saw the sleeping lady's eyes open. The man rushed to her side and the other figure melted into the shadows.

Borghesia hissed and the images in the diamond faded away. Meylyne stared at her.

"What was all that?"

Borghesia reached for the diamond and rolled it between her palms. Its facets glowed red in the fiery mud.

"The lady in the bed was your grandmother and the man was your grandfather—the queen and king of Rose. Your grandmother had been bitten by a snake and was on the verge of death so the king summoned me to suck out the venom as I was the only one who could save her."

"That stranger was *you*?" Meylyne gasped. "But . . . but *how*? I thought snake people couldn't survive in the Above-World."

"Chifflin has always been resourceful. He brought me a person-skin to wear."

Meylyne's eyes widened even further. "A *person-skin?* He would never do that! He'd be too afraid of being eaten for one thing!"

"Oh no. He had something of value for me—something more valuable than his puny life."

Meylyne frowned. As far as she knew, all the snake people wanted from the Above-Worldians was to eat them.

"What?"

"Freedom!" Borghesia's eyes flashed. "He promised me the whereabouts of a grytch to Aardverd, if I spared his life and saved the queen."

"A grytch to Aardverd?"

Meylyne stared at Borghesia, shock and horror mingling in her expression. The snake people couldn't be allowed out of the Beneath-World. They would slaughter everyone. Borghesia stared back at her. It was as if she was reading her mind. Meylyne quickly looked away.

"I see," she said aloud. "So you weren't *biting* my grandmother—you were saving her."

"Yes. And then Chifflin handed me a slip of paper—a map to the tunnel—and sent me on my way. But he tricked me. By the time I arrived home, the map had disappeared—it must have been drawn in vanishing ink."

"Chifflin broke his promise to you?"

Now Meylyne felt even more shocked. As intolerable as it would be to unleash the snake people on the Aardverdians, Glendoch's sage not keeping his word was even worse. Glendoch's sage had to be fair above all else. All order would be lost otherwise.

Borghesia shrugged as she swung her long legs around and underneath her.

"I should have known better—of all the creatures on Glendoch, you humans are the most likely to betray."

She stared at Meylyne with such naked malevolence that Meylyne winced.

"So you kidnapped my mother as revenge?"

"Vengeance?" Borghesia smiled coldly. "No—*justice.* The Roses were in our debt. As they still are."

Understanding dawned on Meylyne. Queen Scarlet's talk of Glendoch being riddled with secrets and righting old wrongs. It all made sense now.

"And in order to repay that debt fully, you must tell me where the grytch to Aardverd is, for a start," Borghesia said.

"A *start?*" As if revealing the location of the grytch wasn't bad enough. "What else do you want?"

"Let us come to that later. It is trivial."

Meylyne dug her fingernails into her palms. She was

trapped. Borghesia was definitely owed the information she wanted. At the same time, there was no way could she give up the grytch.

What happens to the Aardverdians will all be my fault!

"Do not worry about Aardverd," Borghesia said as if reading her mind. "We are not the enemy you think we are."

"Really. So you won't kill me as soon as I've told you?"

Borghesia laughed softly. "Indeed, the human in me would be tempted to do so but the snake would never let me. Your death isn't part of the bargain and we do not stray from *our* code." She leaned back. "So here we are. The measure of Glendoch, past, present, and future held in your hands. What choice will *you* make, Meylyne of Rose?"

Sweat trickled down Meylyne's back and the snakeskin clung damply to her skin. She hated Chifflin for leaving this to her to do.

"It is not just we that will be satisfied once this debt has been settled. *Trisdyan* too will thank you," Borghesia added slyly.

"*Trisdyan?* What do you mean?"

A smile played around Borghesia's lips.

"Have you never wondered how it is that your mother was able to poison the Great Oaken Mother? The tree was after all under Trisdyan's protection."

Meylyne frowned. She hadn't thought of that before.

"Well, *now* I know it was because of the Relic that's possessed her. Obviously it's not of this world. It must be super powerful!"

Borghesia blinked. It was the first time Meylyne had seen her do that.

"Relic? Hmmm."

She fell silent for a second and then shook herself.

"Trisdyan's power knows almost no bounds. No otherworldly spirit could match it. But he made a bad decision the day he let the Roses trick us, and his guilt weighed upon him. It made him vulnerable to the curse under which he molders right now. He cannot shake it off until this wrong has been righted."

"Trisdyan is cursed?" Meylyne gasped.

"How else could things on Glendoch have got so bad?"

Meylyne thought about this. Deep down, she had feared that Trisdyan had simply abandoned them. But he would never do that. This made a lot more sense.

"Fine," she blurted out. "The tunnel to Aardverd is in the Valley of Half-Light—that's where Blue came out."

It was as if the room itself sighed in relief. Borghesia's face stretched into something resembling a smile.

"Thank you, Princess of Rose. You have made the right choice. Maybe there is hope for Glendoch after all."

The patterns in the mud swirled around Meylyne. To her right, a thin pink stripe flickered. She had almost forgotten about the snake that had brought her here.

"No there's not. Didn't your little spy tell you? Glendoch is on the verge of war!"

Borghesia stood up.

"I know that. Now my little *spy,* as you so unfairly name her, will guide you out. Farewell, Princess of Rose."

Meylyne jumped to her feet. "Wait! You said before that telling you about the grytch was just a start to repaying the Rose's debt. What's the rest of it?"

Instead of answering her, Borghesia said, "Why do you not heal the Great Oaken Mother if you wish to save the Above-World from war? It is the sphers that drive your people to fight."

"What do you think I've been trying to do? My mother has Anzulla's feathers! How are we supposed to heal the Great Oaken Mother without those?"

Borghesia laughed.

"Foolish child. You don't need Anzulla's feathers. You have your own."

22

Return to the Above-World

IN THE NEXT SECOND, BORGHESIA WAS GONE.

"Wait—what do you mean?" Meylyne cried.

Silence met her ears. All around her, the patterns in the mud swirled. There was a flicker of pink by her feet.

"Come," the snake said, slithering away.

Meylyne hurried after it and before long they were back in the tunnel. The sentinels were still there, as watchful as ever. Meylyne did her best to ignore their hungry yellow eyes as she sped past.

"Slow down!" she puffed at the snake. "And tell me what she meant about my feathers!"

Still the snake did not answer her, nor did it slow down. It was not until they were back at the gates that it stopped.

"You'll have to leave the snakeskin here," it said.

"Of course I'm going to leave it here! Do you think I want to take it with me?" Meylyne ripped off the suit, all too happy to get the hot, sticky thing away from her skin. "There—now will you tell me about my feathers?"

The snake stared at Meylyne with its piercing blue eyes, once again reminding Meylyne of someone.

"This knowledge comes with the burden of responsibility. If I tell you, your life will never be the same again."

Meylyne snorted. "In case you hadn't noticed, my life is *already* never going to be the same again!"

The snake bowed its head. It seemed to be weighing its words. Then it spoke.

"As all Glendochians know but are so quick to forget, there are rules that govern our worlds. Balance will always be restored. You, through your garlysle side—your feathers that is—have the power to restore balance where it has been unfairly tipped.

Meylyne gave the snake a flat look. "I have no idea what you're talking about."

The snake sighed. "Simply put, your feathers have the power to heal."

"What, like *I* am descended from Trisdyan? No I'm not, that's ridiculous!"

"But remember this," the snake went on. "You may only use your feathers' powers where another's power has been unfairly used. And every time you use them, your strength will be diminished, so use them wisely."

Meylyne opened her mouth, and then closed it again. She didn't know where to start with her questions.

"And you must never, *ever* use them when you're angry. Now you must go, but before you do, I need one of your feathers please."

"What for?"

"It is the completion of your debt to the snake people."

Meylyne hesitated but she knew there'd be no getting out of the Beneath-World otherwise. Reaching around herself, she plucked out a feather and held it out to the snake.

"Tuck it in the band around my neck, please," the snake said.

Meylyne tucked the feather in the band around the snake's neck. It was the color of rose-gold and so thin Meylyne had not noticed it before. A familiar fragrance filled her nose.

"Roses," she murmured. "I've smelled them so many times."

Her eyes widened as the truth dawned on her. "It was you all along, wasn't it? You're the one that magicked us to Grimorex's, and you switched my spell book, didn't you? How long have you been following us? Who *are* you?"

"I, following *you?* Guiding you more like."

The gate slowly swung open. Sunlight poured in, blinding Meylyne and she shielded her eyes against it. When she looked back, the snake was gone.

"Wait! How do I get back to Grimorex's?" she cried.

"Back through the grytch," the snake's voice floated back to her. "Do not delay, Meylyne. Time is not on your side."

"But—"

The gate began to close. Meylyne rushed outside. The last thing she needed was to be stuck in that ghastly place. She made it out just as the gate slammed shut behind her. Sinking to the ground, she relished the cold dawn air as relief flooded her insides like warm treacle.

Then she shot up. How on Glendoch was she going to get back to Grimorex's? Her warm treacle-y feeling turned to ice. Grytchs liked to hide. She could be stuck here forever! She squinted at the crater walls but all she saw were silver roots.

"Do you know where the grytch is?" she asked desperately of those nearest her.

"Other side." She heard the words murmured in her head, low and reedy and bolted to the other side of the crater, wincing as her broken wing gave a sharp twinge.

Stupid snake. My wings don't have the power to heal or restore balance or whatever it said. They can't even heal themselves!

"Am I near the grytch?" she puffed once she had reached the other side of the crater.

There was no answer from the roots.

Placing her hands on the roots, she tried again. Still no answer. Clearly these roots weren't talking. Grytchs had all but disappeared and the few that remained were closely guarded.

While Meylyne fought the urge to throttle the roots, it struck her that she could fly out! There was no telling where she'd end up but at least she'd be out of this stupid crater. Unfurling her wings, she cried out as a sharp pain jabbed into her back. Tears of frustration coursed down her cheeks. There was no way she'd fly anywhere until she had fixed that wing!

"I don't have time for any of this. I need to get *back!*" she cried.

As if in answer, her unbroken wing tugged toward the right.

"What the . . . ?" she murmured, startled.

The wing tugged her again, this time so determinedly that she stumbled sideways. Clearly her wing wanted her to move to the right. She allowed it to lead her, brushing her hands over the roots as she went. A low humming noise rose up before her, just as her wing stopped pulling. Two of the silver roots glowed. Drawing nearer, she saw something that looked a rip in the air between them. Blue light spilled out.

Did my wings just show me where the grytch is?

Swallowing, she reached in her hand and then screamed as all of her was pulled inside. As before she could not tell if she fell or flew. A kaleidoscope of light and sparks whooshed by. She was spat out of the tunnel headfirst, pain searing her back as she landed on all fours.

Icicle-thin shards of sunlight glinted through the tall trees towering all around her. She was back in Grimorex's forest! She had no idea what had just happened but had no time to think about that now. Scrambling to her feet, she closed up her wings. The broken one hurt less that way.

"Which way to the castle?" she panted at the nearest tree.

"That way," it whispered, its branches creaking to the right.

Meylyne sped through the woods. Brambles pulled at her dress and scratched her legs but she didn't notice. Within minutes she burst out of the forest. Grimorex's castle loomed up before her. Grimorex must have seen her coming because he was there in seconds, striding toward her.

"Thank goodness you're safe!" he cried, scooping her up. "We were worried sick when we couldn't find you! Where have you been?"

Meylyne nestled into his velvet jacket and felt she had never been happier to see someone in her life.

"I'll tell you all about it. First let's get Blue and Hope!"

Meylyne felt Grimorex stiffen.

"What?" she demanded. "What's happened?"

"Blue's fine. It's Hope. He's, well, see for yourself."

Grimorex talked nonstop as he strode up his garden. "We thought all was lost. You were on the verge of death. Then you disappeared—and now here you are seeming perfectly fine."

He stopped abruptly in front of a conservatory. Its glass walls were all steamed up. Grimorex pushed open the door and they went in. The air was so warm and humid that at first Meylyne found it hard to breathe.

Then she saw Hope.

He lay in the middle of the room, covered by blankets. His beautiful mane had turned white. Blue was kneeling by his side and he turned when the door opened.

"Meylyne! You're back! Where were you? I looked everywhere for you!"

Meylyne gave him a brief hug and then dropped to Hope's side.

"I'm fine—I'll tell you about it later. What's happened to Hope?"

Blue stared at her for a moment as if he couldn't quite believe his eyes. He shook himself.

"It's the poison from those ghost-wolves. This has been happening for days. Look—"

Blue lifted up a blanket. Not only was Hope's mane white, his coat had turned white too.

"Days? How many days?" Meylyne asked.

"Three—ever since you've been gone."

"Three? But it felt like just a few hours to me!"

Meylyne remembered that grytchs could warp time. Laying a hand on Hope's neck, she was shocked at how cold he was. At the touch of her hand, his eyes fluttered open and then closed again. It was as her mother had said—his heart was almost completely frozen.

"We've *got* to warm him up somehow!"

"We've tried. Nothing has worked," Grimorex said.

Meylyne thought desperately. There must be a way to heal him. The answer was probably in her book somewhere, but it wouldn't be easy to combat the Aethelrix. It could take ages to find. Hope didn't have more than a few minutes by the looks of things.

Sweat trickled down between her shoulder blades. Her wings were too hot. Without thinking, she unfurled them to cool them. Slivers of pain shot through her back.

"Oww!" she said. She'd forgotten about her broken wing. Worst of all, her wings weren't cooling down at all. If anything, they were getting hotter. A thrumming noise reverberated around her and color—*every* color—infused the glass room. A feeling of lightheadedness stole over her. As if from a long way away, she heard Blue gasp,

"What's happening?"

Underneath Meylyne's hand, Hope's neck no longer felt ice-cold. It was warming up. The gray spots were returning to his coat. He stretched and moaned, and then his eyes opened.

"Cold!" he muttered, and started to shiver.

"Get up and walk around!" Grimorex ordered.

Meylyne watched in a daze as Hope slowly pushed himself to his feet. His legs buckled and then held.

"What happen?" he murmured. "Feel like . . . sleeping in fog!"

"You—you're okay!" Blue exclaimed. "We thought you were *dead!* But then Meylyne's wings did this . . . multicolored thing and, like, you're all better!"

Jumping up, he flung his arms around Hope's leg.

"How'd you *do* that?" Blue directed this last question at Meylyne, who sagged against a plant pot with her eyes closed, looking and feeling like a lump of lead.

"It was my wings," she rasped.

"Well yeah but—"

"Wait. It's too hot in here," Grimorex interrupted, looking concernedly at Meylyne. "Are you warm enough to go outside, Hope?"

Hope nodded. Grimorex scooped Meylyne up and the four of them went outside. A smell of roses wafted by her nose and she opened her eyes, looking for the snake. Grimorex's rose-garden was right there. That was all that she had smelled.

"Well?" Blue demanded.

"Give her time!" Grimorex scolded.

Meylyne closed her eyes again. In the distance a pecking bird drilled away. It all seemed so peaceful that her whole encounter with Borghesia felt like a dream.

"I was in the Beneath-World."

Grimorex, Hope, and Blue sat in stunned silence as Meylyne told them everything, from the snake that had been guiding them, to meeting Borghesia and finally to the debt that *she* had had to repay.

"Well I'll be," Grimorex murmured when she had finished. "To think that all this time the Rose's betrayal has been rotting in Glendoch's core. No wonder Glendoch has been plagued with troubles."

"Yeah—troubles that we've been trying to fix, that Meylyne could've fixed all along!" Blue exclaimed. "I mean, seriously? We've been chasing Anzulla, when *your* feathers have the same powers?"

Meylyne managed a weak smile.

"I know! It's like they have a mind of their own when

they're spread out. I'm telling you—they showed me that grytch!" She shifted and groaned as pain shot through her shoulder blades. "I don't see why they can't heal themselves though."

Grimorex stroked his chin. "You're in charge of them, Meylyne. You're going to have to heal them yourself."

Meylyne stared up at him.

"But Anzulla was descended from *Trisdyan!* How would *my* feathers have those sorts of powers?"

Blue rolled his eyes. "Er, well, clearly they do! You healed Hope didn't you?"

"Yes. You fix me, and you can heal Great Oaken Mother, Meylyne." Hope pushed himself to his feet. "And we need go *now.*"

For a second everyone looked at Hope as if he'd sprouted horns.

"Dude, you've just come back from, like, the brink of death. Are you sure you're okay?" Blue asked.

"Never been better. Come!"

"Surely we can wait a few minutes," Meylyne pleaded. The leadenness in her body had lifted. Now she just felt like jelly.

"Not really," Hope replied.

Meylyne eyed him. His tone was a warning.

"Why not?"

For a moment, Hope did not reply. Then he sighed. "Remember before, when I stay behind to search in Diamond Chariot for clues? Well I see Hyldas flying toward Glendoch."

No one said a word. The wind rustled the spiky hollybush leaves and again the smell of roses washed over Meylyne. She thought of the snake. *Time is not on your side,* it had said. Now she knew why—the battle was already on its way.

"Why didn't you say so before?" she demanded.

"No point! Only worry you more. You need mind clear to take on Thorn Queen!"

"He's perfectly right, Meylyne, and there's no time for arguing," Grimorex interrupted. "Let's take the diamond chariot. We'll be in Glendoch by sundown!"

23

Restoring the Balance

MEYLYNE SAT AT THE FRONT OF THE CHARIOT WITH her eyes closed. The others were somewhere behind her, huddling together for warmth. They had set off for Glendoch about an hour ago; a restless wind starting up minutes after they left. It smacked them from all directions, rocking the chariot and whipping Meylyne's hair into rat-tails. Despite all the roiling and lurching, the cold air invigorated her. She opened her eyes to find Hope standing there.

"You angry with me?" he asked, mistaking that as the reason for her aloofness.

Shaking her head, Meylyne told him what the snake had said about her feathers' powers weakening when she used them.

"I feel a bit less mangled now than I did earlier, but what if my wings aren't strong enough to heal the Great Oaken Mother any more?" she finished.

"They will be," Hope said after a moment's consideration. "You only used once. They got lots power. That obvious. Real question—who is snake? What its role in all this?"

At that moment, Blue and Grimorex came over. Grimorex had a platter of dates and cheese, drizzled with honey. He held it out to Meylyne, who grabbed a handful and began munching, smearing honey over her mouth. She hadn't realized how hungry she was.

"Yeah, I've been wondering the same thing," Blue replied, having overheard what Hope had said. "Do you remember how we got magicked here so quickly when we were trying to get to the Valley of Half-Light? It must've been the snake that did that!"

"Yes, and it gave me back my real incantation book," Meylyne replied, licking her sticky fingers.

"How would the snake even have that? I thought you said that book was bound to *you*," Blue said.

Before Meylyne could reply, the chariot flew into a cloud, drenching the four of them. Grimorex bundled them into an alcove, wrapping them with an enormous quilted blanket he had stowed away.

"Many unanswered questions remain," he mused. "I am curious about the Relic that has possessed your mother, Meylyne. Why is it so determined to destroy Glendoch?"

Shrugging, Meylyne felt a sharp twinge in her wing and remembered that it was still fractured. She pulled out her incantation book.

"I don't know but Borghesia said that by giving her the whereabouts to the tunnel to Aardverd, I would also release Trisdyan from his curse. If she was right, then that Relic's got no chance now!"

"Curse? What curse?" Grimorex said sharply.

"I don't know—something to do with how Trisdyan was supposed to keep the balance between light and dark. He wasn't supposed to let the Roses deceive Borghesia like they did, and he got cursed as a result."

Grimorex stared at her for a minute.

"Cursed by whom? Although that would certainly explain how your mother was able to poison the Great Oaken Mother—Trisdyan wasn't around to protect her."

An idea occurred to Meylyne and she grabbed Grimorex's wrist.

"Do you think Trisdyan's around now? Because then he could heal the Great Oaken Mother! I'd be off the hook, right?"

"Wrong—we are not going to count on that," Blue retorted.

"I'm afraid he's right, Meylyne. Trisdyan has been absent a long time. We really can't count on his presence now," Grimorex said.

Deflated, Meylyne folded her arms and another sharp pain stabbed into her shoulder blade. She really had to mend those snapped bones. Scooting out from underneath the blanket, she unfurled her wings.

"Fine. Whatever. Now if you'll excuse me for a minute, I need to fix this broken wing of mine," she muttered, flicking through the pages of her book. "This should be a pretty basic healing spell—it's just a Level Three. For everyone's sake, I hope it works."

Eyeing the others, she moved back a little further. It wouldn't do to catch them in the crosswind of her incantation. She murmured the words from her book, all the while focusing her thoughts on her wing and nothing but her wing. There was a series of ripples and pops as the delicate bones fused together.

An incredulous smile spread over her face.

"It's *working!* I can actually feel my wing mending. I love this Book of Incantations! Look!"

She stretched out her wing for her friends to see.

"Wow—check that out," Blue marveled. "All better!"

"Well done Meylyne," Hope said admiringly.

Grimorex, however, was miles away. Meylyne prodded him.

"Grimorex, look!"

"What? Oh yes, very good."

Meylyne frowned. He was obviously still distracted. Before she could find out why, however, the chariot emerged from the clouds. Now the air was still and warm. The wind must have found someone else to torment. Scrambling to their feet, the friends ran to the front of the chariot.

"It's Glendoch!" Meylyne cried.

The sun-drenched glacier sparkled like an enormous diamond. Its golden Titons shimmered and, beyond them the bridge to the Valley of Half-Light twisted and turned like a giant snake. Meylyne remembered the last time they were there. It felt like a lifetime ago.

"Wow—we're almost there!" Blue said. He bit his cheek and a troubled look stole over his face. "You know, assuming that Trisdyan hasn't made a miraculous reappearance, then that tree mother will have gotten sicker, in which case more sphers will have escaped. They could be all around her now."

Meylyne paled. Healing the Great Oaken Mother would be hard enough—she didn't need an army of sphers to battle too.

"Oh sweet Trisdyan," Grimorex murmured.

"I know! That's the last thing we need—"

"No—look!" Grimorex interrupted Meylyne.

Her eyes followed his gaze to a spot in the distance,

where they rested upon a decrepit, dying tree. Dread swelled inside her like a lead balloon.

"Is that—?"

"Yes," Grimorex replied. "That is the Great Oaken Mother."

The color of ash, the Great Oaken Mother had no leaves left at all and the few branches that remained drooped to the ground. But what was worse was the cloud of smoke—or at least what looked like smoke—that hung around her.

"Are . . . are those sphers?" Blue gasped.

Meylyne nodded. "There's no saving her now. We're too late." Tears pricked at the back of her eyes. Then she jumped as Blue smacked her on the shin.

"It is not too late! This is the perfect opportunity for you to use your wings. Don't you see? That whole 'restoring the balance' thing? Now is the time for that! Those sphers are no match against you!"

Meylyne blinked at him. No match against her? Her wing still ached and her bones felt like sand. She wasn't sure she could fly, let alone fight off sphers *and* save the tree while she was at it.

"It's too risky. One or two sphers would be a problem. That—" Grimorex pointed at the wall of sphers. "—is a non-starter."

"How can you say that? You saw what her wings did to Hope!" Blue cried. "We didn't come this far to give up like this!" He clutched Meylyne's arm. "I'll go with you—you can fly me on your back!"

Meylyne shook her head. "I'm not sure I can fly at all. I don't need you on my back as well!"

"Well try at least! And fast—we don't have all day here!"

Meylyne swallowed. Blue was right. They were out of time and out of options.

Hope nudged her arm and she turned to face him. His eyes bore into hers. Of all of them, he knew her the best.

"What you think, Meylyne—you up to it?" he asked, watching her closely.

"If I can fly off this chariot, then yes—"

"Atta girl!"

Blue slapped her again and she winced at how it jarred her. At this rate, she'd say her chances were fifty-fifty. Judging by the dubious looks on Hope's and Grimorex's faces, they felt the same way.

"But I'm not taking you with me! I mean it." She held up her finger to stop Blue from protesting. "If I can fly myself off this chariot it will be a miracle. I'll never do it with you on my back."

"But—"

"No."

Climbing up on the side of the chariot, Meylyne took a last look at her friends. Blue's mouth was set in a grim line. Grimorex's eyes glistened with tears. Only Hope looked calm.

"We right behind you. If you start fall, chariot catch you," he said.

"Yes, and remember, it's not just your wings that must be strong—it is also your mind. Sphers prey upon fear. When they invade your thoughts, recall the ones you love," Grimorex said, his voice catching.

Nodding, Meylyne unfurled her wings. She was only half listening. If she was going to do this, she had to do it now before she completely lost her nerve.

Taking a deep breath, she pushed her wing muscles down.

The air pushed back and in a flash she was above the chariot. Lifting her knees, she dove down toward the tree, soaring with the wind like the paper airplanes she used to make. Once again, the air was holding her up.

Despite the dire circumstances, exhilaration flooded her, suffusing her muscles with energy all the way to her fingers and toes. If her wings could fly, they could heal the Great Oaken Mother, she was sure of it! She headed toward the tree and crashed head first into the wall of spheres.

Everything changed. Her strength vanished. Her confidence shriveled. All she felt now was a gripping terror, as if she had plunged into a pit of hairy spiders. The wispy beings wound around her and worse, *through* her. She opened her mouth to scream and gagged at the putrid taste of decay and rot. Retching, she tried to fly away but her wings felt like they were trapped in glue. She could not get out.

Then the images seeped into her mind—her mother waiting for her on the bed, smiling as she admitted she had deceived Meylyne her whole life . . .

Meylyne moaned. Dread, cold and sick spread throughout her like mold. Grimorex had warned her about this. She tried to remember what he had said but it was as if her mind was full of fungus.

I should have listened better. She stifled a sob. *Dear Grimorex with his thigh-high boots and his love of life . . . all his hidden goodness . . .*

Through the suffocating misery her wings tingled. Just a fraction but it was all she needed. In a flash, Grimorex's words came back to her.

Recall the ones you love.

The images were hazy at first. Slowly they came together. Hope with his brown, loyal eyes. Blue, always smiling. *Trin and Train—the happiness on their faces when she finally saw them again ...*

Everything that happened next was a blur. Energy like lightening crackled through her wings. The gray fog turned red. Sphers writhed and shrieked, glowing like embers and then falling away . . .

Through the waning mist, Meylyne caught sight of the Great Oaken Mother. She flew to it, her wings pulsing with alchemy as she wrapped them around its trunk. Her stomach lurched—

The tree is tipping over!

The Great Oaken Mother howled in agony as her enormous roots ripped up from the ground. Meylyne shrieked. A vision came into her mind—*a giant hand rising up from the earth, catching the tree before it fell.*

A shower of red sparks shot down from her wings. The tree gathered speed and Meylyne braced herself for the crash . . .

. . . that never came.

Looking down, Meylyne saw that something had grabbed the tree by its trunk. At first she thought it was the tree's own roots but then she realized it was other trees' roots, curled around its trunk like giant fingers. With a great deal of creaking and groaning, the Great Oaken Mother slowly stood upright again.

As she heard the sounds of cheering from above, her world went topsy-turvy. Next thing she knew she was sprawled on the ground like a glob of pudding. Beside her, the trunk pulsed with life.

"Thank you Meylyne," whispered the Great Oaken Mother. "I *knew* you could heal me!"

Meylyne mustered up her strength to reply but could only mumble incoherently. She managed to sit up as footsteps crunched toward her.

"You did it Meylyne!"

Skidding across the ice, Blue almost landed on her lap. "You healed the Tree-Mother! I *knew* you could. You saved Glendoch!"

A smile flickered over Meylyne's face but then she heard the tree sigh. Something was wrong.

"What?" she rasped.

"I'm afraid your work is not quite done. You have healed me, it is true, but you have not yet saved Glendoch. War still brews," the Great Oaken Mother murmured. "You must hasten to Glendoch's Wishing Well before it is too late!"

Grimorex and Hope appeared at her side, Grimorex beaming from ear to ear.

"Well done—" he started but Meylyne cut him off.

"Save it," she wheezed. "Not done. Great Oaken Mother says still a chance of war. Must go to the Wishing Well. Now!"

She tried to push herself to her feet but her limbs refused to move.

"I can't—"

Grabbing her arms, Grimorex lifted her into the air and slung her over his shoulder.

"Come on! I had a feeling this would happen. Back to the chariot. It will get us to the Wishing Well in no time."

"Wait! Why? What's happening at the well?" Blue panted, running behind them.

Grimorex leapt aboard the chariot.

"We'll find out soon enough!""

24

The Peaceweaver

GLENDOCH'S WISHING WELL WAS ANCIENT. NESTLED between the mountains ringing the east side of Glendoch Proper, rumor had it that all Glendoch had been born from wishes thrown into it. Over the years, the well had filled with snow and all that remained was a ring of stones protruding from the ice like broken teeth. Hardly anyone visited there any more, even though the frozen lake behind it was perfect for ice skating. It was too close to the Outlands for people to feel safe there, except for those days when a special occasion drew a crowd.

Today was one of those days. Hundreds of Glendochians were gathered around the well, Tyrians to one side, Francescans to another. A cloud of tense anticipation hung around them while the sun beat down upon their heads from an azure, cloudless sky. Sweat trickled down their necks and pockets of midges buzzed around their shoulders, biting uncovered patches of skin. Without a breeze, it was as if the air itself was waiting.

At the center of it all stood the royals and their guards. All wore their house uniforms—the crimson and turquoise silks a sharp contrast to the blur of colors around them. Looking stiff in her Cardinal House garb, Queen Emery read from a roll of parchment, her voice high and strained.

"You know we have searched for many years for a Rose peaceweaver to unite our two houses and put all this strife to rest. We are crushingly aware that many of you have suffered as—"

Queen Emery stopped in the middle of her speech.

Prince Piam, standing to her right, peered at her from underneath his helmet.

"Go on Mother! People are waiting!" he hissed.

Her eyes were riveted on a spot in the sky.

"I know Piam but look—do you see that speck in the distance? What *is* that?"

"I'm sure it's nothing. Oh—hang on, I do see it! It looks like... a giant *prism* or something—"

As he trailed off, the crowd became a sea of upturned faces as everyone craned their necks to see what held the royals' attention.

"What's that?" someone screamed, pointing toward the sky.

"It's a dragon!" another voice yelled. *"Run for it!"*

Within seconds, the crowd erupted into a mass of shrieks and flailing limbs as people dashed in all directions, tripping over and barreling into each other. Those that ran at the royals got shoved back from the guards.

"Order!" they roared. *"Order!"*

No one paid them any notice. Prince Piam grabbed the megaphone from the queen.

"Everyone calm down! Stay where you are! It is *not* a dragon. There is no need to panic. I repeat—"

A low whining noise filled the air. Piam snapped up his head just in time to see the enormous prism-like object shoot straight toward him and his mother.

"Yaaaahhhhh!" he yelled, throwing himself before Queen Emery. Huge chunks of ice hurtled through the air as the object smashed into the frozen lake. Piam grunted, flying forward as one of the chunks thudded into his back.

"Piam!" Queen Emery screamed and rushed toward him.

Piam pushed himself to his feet, grimacing.

"I'm fine. Stay back. You—" he jabbed his finger at a mounted guard. "Come with me."

Drawing his sword, Piam approached the lake. Light streamed off the gigantic, sparkling object wedged into the broken ice. He and the guard halted in their tracks as three blurry shapes and what looked like a tall, thin tree emerged from the dazzling blaze. Prince Piam blinked as they came into focus.

"Hold it right there! Identify yourselves!"

The diamond chariot had wasted no time in getting Meylyne, Blue, Grimorex and Hope to the Wishing Well. When the well came into view, the chariot pointed its nose down and hurtled toward it like a comet. Pulling up at the last minute did not save them from skidding into the lake, and everyone landed on Grimorex amidst a cloud of ice shards.

"Sweet Trisdyan have mercy," Grimorex groaned, pushing Hope off his stomach.

"Come on! We've no time to waste!" Blue cried, bounding off the chariot.

Grimacing, Meylyne clung to Hope for support as they

stumbled after Blue. She had regained some of her energy, but she still felt like someone had pummeled her with rocks.

Blue waited for them to catch up.

"Who's that?" he growled, pointing ahead at two figures that had emerged from the icy rubble. Both wore the Cardinal House uniform of turquoise and gold. One was waving his sword and bellowing. Meylyne caught her breath as she recognized him.

Prince Piam! The last time she'd seen him he had been squashed underneath her.

"That Prince Piam," Hope said.

"Oh right. The one Meylyne flattened. This should go well." Blue rested his hand on the hilt of his sword "What's he saying?"

Meylyne shook her head. It was impossible to tell. Her ears still rang from the flight and the shrieking, fleeing crowd didn't help.

Prince Piam inched closer.

"You have three seconds to state your purpose before I set my guards on you!" Piam roared.

This time the friends understood what he said. A line of guards clambered over the chunks of ice. From what Meylyne could see, there were about fifty of them. Bile rose in her throat.

"It's me, Meylyne!" she rasped, her voice weak and wobbly. "Please—you must listen to us! This—"

"Meylyne? The one that *fell* on me?" Piam interrupted. He sounded more shocked than outraged.

Two figures pushed their way between the row of guards to join Prince Piam. It was Queen Emery and Chifflin. When the queen saw Meylyne her eyes almost popped out of her head.

"*Meylyne,*" she gasped. "You. Have. Wings."

"Yes, that's what matters Mother," Prince Piam snapped. Then he yelled, "Seize them!"

The guards charged. Meylyne balled up her fists, ready to fling a wind-shield around her friends and herself but Blue whirled around with such agility and speed that it seemed to Meylyne he had ten blades, not one. His size made him near-impossible to see. Within seconds, half of the guards were disarmed and on their backs. A few kicks from Grimorex sent the others flying.

"Look, just listen to Meylyne for a minute," Blue panted as Prince Piam leveled his sword at him. "You can stop this war right now!"

For a second there was silence, broken only by the faint rustling of leaves in the cedars beyond. The guards got to their feet but kept their distance.

"Who are *you*? And what *war* are you talking about?" Piam demanded.

Meylyne opened her mouth to speak and then closed it again. Prince Piam and Queen Emery seemed remarkably calm considering they were about to go to war. For the first time, she took a good look at the few members of the crowd that had not fled and were peering curiously at them from behind the guards.

No swords. No battle armor. What's going on?

Then she spotted the girl all dressed in white. She wore the traditional headgear of a bride.

Why would a bride be here unless—

"Is, is this a *wedding?*" she asked incredulously.

"Of course it is! What did you think? This is *my* wedding

and you're not going to stop it, as much as you'd like to. We're finally going to unite the Houses of Cardinal and Rose," Prince Piam replied.

Meylyne blinked. "You found a Rose peaceweaver?"

The girl in white moved forward until she stood inside the Wishing Well. Tresses of chestnut-brown hair cascaded down her back and her skin was the color of freshly-fallen snow. She smiled timidly at Meylyne and as she did so Meylyne saw something move inside her big blue eyes—something scrabbling to get out.

Just like Mother's eyes.

Comprehension dawned upon Meylyne. *This* was the war that the Great Oaken Mother had spoken of. With her mother poisoning Prince Piam's mind, Glendoch would end in bloodshed just as surely as if it were overrun with sphers. With a mirthless chuckle she said, "Very clever Mother."

Meylyne turned back to Piam. "Listen to me. You can't marry this girl." She jabbed her finger toward the bride. "She's a *warweaver*, not a peaceweaver. All she wants is to do is destroy Glendoch!"

"Forgive me for stating the obvious," Chifflin interjected. "That girl is *not* your mother, Meylyne—she's a Rose Royal."

Meylyne pursed her lips.

"That she is—but not who you think. How did you so conveniently find yourself a peaceweaver after all this time?"

"I've been living at sea with my uncle," the girl's voice rang out like birdsong.

"What? Oh that's a *great* story!" Meylyne turned back to Prince Piam. "Look, she's not your bride—she's my mother, and furthermore, she's *Princess Amber's sister!*"

There was a moment's silence. Then Queen Emery spoke.

"No, Meylyne—Princess Amber's sister died at birth as everyone knows."

"She didn't die at birth! Her parents, and *you*—" Meylyne stabbed her finger at Chifflin, "—sold her out to the snake people!"

Queen Emery bit her lip and her expression changed from curiosity to pity.

"I'm sure you'd love to consider yourself part of the royal family."

Meylyne threw up her arms.

"Listen! You *must* believe me—"

"Prove it," Chifflin interrupted her.

"Chifflin! Don't encourage her!" said Queen Emery.

"Go on, prove it," Chifflin repeated, ignoring Queen Emery.

The imposter-bride moved behind Prince Piam. "Don't let her hurt me," she whimpered.

"She wouldn't dare," Prince Piam growled. "Why *are* you encouraging her?" he snapped at Chifflin. "I know you had your misgivings about this wedding but—"

Chifflin held up his finger, silencing Prince Piam. His eyes were trained on Meylyne. "We're waiting."

Meylyne squeezed her eyes shut, trying to think. How could she prove it? Her strength was slowly returning but there were too many people around to engage her mother in sorcery without putting them all at risk.

"Call wand to you!" Hope said.

All of the royals jumped. None of them had met a Talking Animal before.

"Did that stallyinx just speak?" Prince Piam asked.

Ignoring him, Meylyne glared at the girl. "It's not that easy. She's not just going to part with it, are you Mother?"

The girl whimpered again.

"I don't know what she's talking about, I swear!"

An idea came to Meylyne. Muttering a single word, she felt the pull of her incantation, drawing her mother's wand to her. It had to be on her somewhere. As she expected, she felt her mother tug the wand back to herself. Turning her palm upward, Meylyne directed the pewter shield in her hand toward the tug, hoping to reverse the energy flow.

It worked! There was a flash of black at the girl's wrist as something hidden up her sleeve shot out toward Meylyne. The girl's hand closed around it, quick as a flash.

Chifflin pointed at it.

"What's that?"

"That's her wand. Why don't you ask her for it?" Meylyne said.

Prince Piam held out his hand to his bride. "May I see that?"

Prince Piam's beautiful bride gave him a look of such malevolence that he backed away. Out of the corner of her eye, Meylyne saw the curious crowd inching nearer. Panic swelled within her.

"Grimorex—move the crowd away."

Grimorex strode toward the crowd, which immediately turned and fled. Meanwhile, the imposter-bride's hair was slowly turning black. She gave a low laugh.

"Well-played Meylyne," she said and her voice was no longer high and clear. Rich and velvety, it was unmistakably that of Meylyne's mother.

"Ellenyr, is that you?" Queen Emery whispered.

By the time the so-called peaceweaver turned to face Queen Emery, the transformation was complete. Queen Emery gasped to see Meylyne's mother in her place.

The air seemed to stand still. Piam's sword hung limply by his side and Chifflin's eyes were like two saucers in his head. Finally Meylyne's mother spoke, splitting the silence with her words.

"Don't call me Ellenyr. My name is Anastisse."

25

Facing the Thorn Queen

"*ANASTISSE*," CHIFFLIN BREATHED. "WE ALL ASSUMED you were dead."

Meylyne's mother shot Chifflin a venomous look and she slashed her wand downward. From the swath it cut in the air flew a swarm of black wasps that dove at Chifflin with a menacing whine. Hope shoved him out of the way just in time. Grabbing a handful of snow, Meylyne flung it at them. It opened into a net, trapping them on the ground.

Meylyne's mother laughed as Chifflin scrambled to his feet.

"Yes of course. You believed what you wanted to believe." Her nostrils flared. "You are Glendoch's sage! *You* were supposed to be the wise one. The *trustworthy* one. Is it any wonder Glendoch is so corrupt?"

To her right, Prince Piam slowly raised his sword. Meylyne's mother flicked her wand and he cried out, dropping his sword to the ground. A large red blister bubbled up on his palm where the sword had scorched him.

"I advise everyone to stay still. I don't want to hurt anyone," said Meylyne's mother.

The crowd became like statues.

"Yes you do," Meylyne retorted. "That's why you unleashed

the sphers. You wanted everyone to kill each other! Why even bother? Why not just do it yourself?"

Meylyne's mother remained silent, her face revealing nothing. From the stones of the Wishing Well, Meylyne heard a whisper—

"She can't. Not without suffering the consequences."

A murder of crows cawed to one another, circling in the air.

"Of course," Meylyne murmured. "The whole balance of power thing. You can't hurt the Glendochians yourself—not if you want to keep the balance in your favor."

Her mother produced a cold smile.

"I wish to reform Glendoch. You, too, have suffered imprisonment—forced to live in the Between-World, treated like an abomination, all because you have garlysle blood. Why don't you join me?"

"Reform Glendoch into *what?* Its cities burned to the ground? The Above-Worldians killed by each other's hand? That's your idea of a reformed Glendoch?"

"At least then it will be honest."

Meylyne squared her shoulders. "No."

Her mother held her gaze and once again Meylyne saw something trying to claw its way out of her eyes.

"How sweet. You thought that was a request."

As her mother lifted her wand, Meylyne stepped inside the Wishing Well and spun around, whistling at the stones surrounding them. Creaking and groaning, they grew as tall as trees, enclosing her and her mother.

Something whizzed by her nose and her mother shrieked. An arrow had pierced her arm. Horrified, Meylyne realized where it had come from.

Oh no—Blue's in here too!

Raising his bow, Blue let fly another arrow. Meylyne's mother ducked. Snarling, she beat her wand in the air. A drop of red liquid fell out, forming into a hideous creature. It looked like an overgrown, hairless cat. Blue backed away, pulling out his dagger just as it pounced on him, sinking its teeth into his neck. Grunting, Blue fell over backward, slashing at the creature with his dagger. It went limp, jagged icicles sprouting from its wound. Blue cried out as one stabbed him in the side.

"Blue!" Meylyne screamed as he lay still on the ground, his eyes closed. Anguish pressed against her lungs, making it hard to breathe. Running to him, she shook his shoulders but he did not wake up.

"I didn't want to hurt him," she heard her mother say. "It's just what happens when alchemists make friends with the ordinary. That's why I stunted your alchemical skills—I wanted you to have the chance at a normal childhood."

Rage bubbled up inside Meylyne.

"How dare you pretend that you did that for *me?* That was all for you, and you know it!"

Pointing at the ice around her mother's feet, she raised up her hand, drawing up a cage of jagged stalagmites around her mother. One pierced her mother's hand and she screamed but still did not drop her wand. It was as if it was a part of her.

Then something fell from the sky. Meylyne looked up. *Hail.* Another one fell, and another. The tiny stones hammered down upon her head and shoulders. She turned her palm to face them and the shower stopped. For a second the hailstones flew up, and then she directed them with all her might toward her mother. They slammed into her wand arm and this time it worked.

With a shriek, her mother dropped the wand. She immediately fell to the ground and tried to pick it up but it was soon buried in hail. She tried to get up but the jagged little rocks bore relentlessly down upon her. Soon she too would be buried.

Meylyne heard her mother's voice carrying over the storm.

"It feels good, doesn't it? All that power to get back at those that hurt you."

Meylyne closed her eyes. Her arms felt like lead—almost too heavy to lift but from the fury that burned in her belly she drew a different sort of strength. It flowed through her like molten lava. Black shapes danced and leaped before her eyes as she directed the fire up toward the hail. It pounded her mother with an even greater ferocity than before.

"But have you forgotten your friend?" Her mother's muffled voice came again. "If you don't heal him soon, he'll be gone."

Blue!

Keeping the sheet of hail pointed at her mother, she looked back at him. He was still lying on the ground, in arm's distance. She could just reach back with one wing to heal him . . .

A sliver of pink slithered by. She heard a hiss—

"Stop, Meylyne, before it is too late."

The snake was there! Suddenly its parting words came back to her—

"Never use your wings while you are angry."

The black shapes continued to twist around her. For a

second the ice-cold fire fueling her subsided and she fell to her knees. The hailstorm lessened.

"No," she snarled, pushing herself to her feet. "Go away snake. I have to use my wings' magic—I must save Blue. She's only getting she gets what she deserves!"

"Then you are just like she."

"*What?* I am nothing like she is!"

"Really? Look behind you."

Meylyne whirled around. The hail had beaten a sheen into one of the boulders. From it, her reflection stared back at her. Wild-eyed with her hair strewn around her blotched face, she barely recognized herself. The tip of the boulder crumbled and Meylyne felt like a piece of her crumbled with it. She hung her head and her wings fell to her sides.

I am doing exactly what my mother wants.

The hailstorm ebbed to a trickle.

"I'm not doing this Mother. I am *not* joining you," she said.

The pile of stones covering her mother fell away as she stood up. Plunging her hands into the rubble before her, she pulled out her wand.

"Yes. You. WILL!"

The blows came out of nowhere. Next thing she knew, Meylyne was on her back, the breath knocked out of her. She heard Blue's voice and then everything happened at once . . . a flash of steel . . . his sword clattering beside her . . . a shadow above. Rolling to her side, she grabbed the sword and swung it. An explosion of black and gold sparks showered down around her.

The silence that followed seemed to stretch for an eternity.

Is this what death is? Meylyne wondered.

Then a howl slashed through the silence like a scythe. Through the thinning sparkles, Meylyne saw her mother crouched on the ground, staring at something.

Her wand—slashed in two!

Her mother howled again, gathering the wand's pieces to her. Meylyne tried to get up but slabs of boulder pinned her down. One must have shattered on her. With a roar, she heaved a piece off her legs and crawled to where her mother sat.

"Mother—"

"*You're no daughter of mine!*" her mother spat in a strangled voice as her face twisted in agony. The wand's pieces glowed and her mother shrieked as the skin on her face and arms went gray and grainy and then—

POOF!!!

Meylyne's brain refused to register what her eyes saw.

Her mother had burst into a cloud of dust.

Shrieking like a chorus of banshees, the dust cloud reared up and shot down toward Meylyne. She ducked and it shot over her head. With a final howl, it divided in half and disappeared into the wand's two halves.

Meylyne edged away. She half expected her mother to reemerge but as the seconds turned into minutes she became aware of the stillness settling upon her and she knew her mother would not come back.

Something glinted on the ground next to the broken wand. She picked it up.

Mother's black opal.

Then the world tilted and the sound receded into silence as everything around Meylyne went black.

26

Homecoming

MEYLYNE EMERGED INTO A WORLD OF SHADOWS.

Wherever she was, it was like lying in a cloud. A candle sputtered above her. Golden geese, stitched into the covers over her glinted in its light. She shifted and then froze as something flickered in the gloom.

"Who's there?" she croaked.

There was a flash of pink and the snake slithered into the candlelight. Meylyne gazed at it, still trying to put all the pieces together when the floodgates of her mind opened. Images of everything that had happened crashed into her thoughts—*Blue's sword hurtling toward her, the wand slashed in half, her mother disappearing inside it ...*

She closed her eyes as a wave of dizziness overcame her.

"Here."

The snake nosed a glass of water toward her.

Meylyne gulped it down. Water had never tasted so delicious before. She opened her eyes but it was impossible to see more than shapes in the gloom beyond the enormous bed in which she lay.

"Where am I?"

"Glendoch Castle."

Glendoch Castle?

While Meylyne struggled to digest this, the snake wiggled around and then nudged something toward her with its nose. It was the rose-gold band it had worn around its neck.

"Put it on," said the snake.

Still in a daze, Meylyne slid her hand through the band and then the room exploded with light. Crying out, she shielded her eyes.

"Turn that off, it's far too bright," a voice scolded. "I'll open the drapes instead."

The glittering blaze disappeared and Meylyne heard footsteps padding into the room. There was a rattling noise and the room brightened—a bedroom by the looks of things, and a gargantuan one at that. She was vaguely aware of ornate dressers and gilded chairs, and a magnificent chandelier hanging above her. A figure appeared by her bedside and she gasped as its features swam into focus.

"Great-Uncle Groq!"

Her great-uncle glared at her as he always did but he laid his talons on her wrist in a caring sort of way. Meylyne was getting over the shock of seeing him when Queen Emery appeared by his side. Meylyne shrank back as the queen leaned toward her, long red hair splashing down over her shoulders.

"How do you feel Meylyne?" she asked.

Tongue-tied, Meylyne could only shrug. She immediately wished she hadn't. It felt like a shower of daggers had pierced her shoulders. Everything hurt. Luckily, she was saved from answering as yet another person bustled in—a nurse, judging by her outfit and the smell of disinfectant that accompanied her. She reached over and felt Meylyne's forehead.

"She's no temperature anyway. No infection anywhere as far as I can see. Just a lot of bruises and a broken foot."

"Thank you, Millie. If you could give us a moment now," Queen Emery said.

Millie scowled. "Don't tire her!"

Meylyne blinked. She could not believe anyone would talk to Queen Emery that way.

"Millie is my old nurse," Queen Emery explained, smiling.

Meylyne blinked again. *Is she smiling at me?*

Then Queen Emery licked her lips, as if she wasn't sure what to say next.

"Do you remember what happened?"

Meylyne nodded. Both her great-uncle and Queen Emery looked at her, clearly waiting for her to say more but she couldn't. She didn't know what to say.

"I can't imagine how you must feel. I, that is we," Queen Emery glanced at Groq, "are so *very* thankful for all that you have done for us."

"You're *thankful?*" Meylyne peered at her great-uncle. "I'm not in trouble?"

Her great-uncle shook his head.

"Not at all. What you did was very brave. I am proud of you. And your father would have been proud of you."

Meylyne's eyebrows shot up to hear him speak of Meph in front of Queen Emery like that. The subject of her father was as welcome as yellow-oozing-scab disease in the palace.

"We know now that it was Anastisse, not your father that was behind Glendoch's troubles," Queen Emery added.

Meylyne's chest tightened at the mention of her mother.

Another memory crashed into her mind—*jagged icicles stabbing Blue—*

A jolt of horror coursed through her. "What about Blue? Is he okay?"

"Oh yes. He is here, in fact, in the castle with Piam."

"Trin and Train are here too—they're all waiting for you to wake up," Groq added.

"Trin and Train are *here?*" Meylyne's eyes darted from Groq to Queen Emery. "In the Above-World? In the *castle?*"

"Yes, they are." Queen Emery smoothed an imaginary crease in her skirt. "We're changing the border rules. Soon, all garlysles and humans may go where they please."

Meylyne gaped at her great-uncle. It was what he had wanted for so long. His feathers puffed up and his glare lessened, which Meylyne knew to be his version of a smile.

"Yes, we can't very well keep the two worlds separate any more. Not now that our next Rose queen is a garloch," he said gruffly.

Meylyne stared at him, trying to make sense of his words. A burning in her lungs told her she needed to breathe. Was he talking about *her?*

"Don't worry," Queen Emery said quickly. "I'm sure it's all far too much to imagine right now. And no one is going to force you to do anything you don't want to do—"

She trailed off, glancing at the door where a small commotion had sprung up. Voices clamored—

"She's awake, isn't she?"

"Yes, and under no circumstances are you going in!"

"*Please!* Just five minutes?"

"Come *on!*"

Meylyne's heart leaped. There was no mistaking the voices of Blue, Trin, and Train.

"Please let them in. I'm fine, really!" she pleaded.

Queen Emery and her great-uncle exchanged a look.

"All right, but not for long. We'll be back later. Just pull this cord if you need anything," Queen Emery said.

She and Meylyne's great-uncle walked away. With a great deal of grunting and groaning, Meylyne maneuvered herself into a sitting position as Blue, Trin, and Train darted into the room. Prince Piam strolled in behind them. Blue leapt up onto her bed while Trin, Train and Prince Piam clustered around it. Everyone's voices jumbled together.

"*Finally*, you're awake!"

"We've missed you *so* much!"

"How do you feel?"

This last question was from Train, who engulfed her in a cloud of red-gold feathers as she sat down next to her. Meylyne squeezed her back as tightly as she could, wincing from the sharp pains slicing through her body. Despite this, she felt ridiculously happy for the first time in ages. As she buried her face in Train's chest, she felt it grow wet with tears.

"Great now that you are all here," she choked.

"You don't look great," Prince Piam remarked, grinning.

Meylyne blushed furiously. She was sure she looked dreadful.

"Don't listen to him. He's just jealous." Blue lifted up his shirt to show a large bandage wrapped around his chest. "I'm going to have such a cool scar from this!"

An image of the demon-cat flitted into Meylyne's mind

and she shuddered. Beads of sweat trickled down her face. She wiped her forehead with the back of her hand and as she did Trin leaned forward.

"Is—is that our mother's shield?" he squawked. "*Melted* into your hand?"

Meylyne had forgotten that the shield was now fused to the palm of her hand. Nodding, she told everyone how she had used it to reverse the incantations flung at her.

"But don't worry—I'll work out a way to give it back to you," she assured Trin and Train.

"No you won't!"

"It belongs to you now," Trin and Train said at the same time.

"Yeah I'd say there's no parting with that," Prince Piam said. "Can I see it again?"

As Meylyne showed it to him the rose-gold band slid down by her hand. Frowning, he grabbed her wrist.

"Where did you get that?"

Meylyne told him about the snake and how it had given it to him. Something told her to leave out the part about the snake being there in the room with them.

"No way," Piam breathed when she had finished. "My mother has the exact same bracelet! It's one of a pair—the other was given to Princess Amber! This could mean she's still alive somewhere." He ran his fingers through his already tousled hair. "Should I tell her? I don't want to get her hopes up if it's not true. She *longs* for Princess Amber. She's desperate to believe she's still alive somewhere!"

Meylyne stared at him. Before she could reply, he jumped up. "It's no use—I have to tell her!"

Prince Piam dashed off, bumping into Nurse Millie as he ran out of the room. "Sorry!"

"You *will* be sorry. How many times have I told you not to run in the castle?" Nurse Millie waddled over to Meylyne's bed, red-faced and muttering.

"Right, that's quite enough excitement for now. Off with all of you! You can spend more time with her tomorrow but for now she needs to eat and rest!"

Deaf to their protests and pleas, she herded Trin, Train, and Blue out of the room. Moments later she reappeared with a steaming bowl of soup. Smells of garlic and ginger wafted toward Meylyne.

"Eat this, get some sleep, and next morning I reckon you'll feel as right as rain!"

Nurse Millie plumped up the pillow behind Meylyne's head, closed the drapes in the room and then left. Meylyne waited a few minutes until she was quite sure that Nurse Millie was nowhere nearby. Then she called out, "Snake? Are you still here?"

There was a rustling noise as the snake slithered out from underneath the bed. It sat, coiled up on the floor, staring at Meylyne with its startlingly blue eyes that had always looked familiar to Meylyne.

Now she knew why.

"Yes I am," the snake hissed. "There's one more thing I need to give you."

Meylyne folded her arms. "How did you get past the seerwolves guarding the castle grounds?"

The snake did not reply.

"I've heard they can sense *anything* out of place—even a worm," Meylyne added.

Still the snake remained silent.

"And I know it takes time to develop a seerwolf's trust," Meylyne persisted. She paused, holding the snake's gaze. "Then again, it would be easy for someone that *grew up* here, wouldn't it?"

Now it was Meylyne who fell silent, waiting for the snake to reply. Outside the window, a lark trilled to its neighbor. After a moment, the snake sighed.

"Oh this is all so *tight.* Give me a second to change into something more comfortable."

Tucking its head down, the snake shivered and wobbled as though possessed. Meylyne gasped as its scaly skin fell away and four limbs stretched out of its body. The pink stripe billowed into a pink dress. When it straightened up, Meylyne found herself staring into two blue eyes and the face of a woman not unlike her mother's. Or her own for that matter.

"*Princess Amber,*" Meylyne breathed.

Although she had guessed the snake's identity, it was still a shock to see the long-lost princess after all she had heard about her.

The young woman stumbled as she moved toward Meylyne's bed. "Ooops! It's been a while since I have walked on two legs."

Sitting on the edge of Meylyne's bed, she held up her finger as Meylyne opened her mouth to speak.

"Sshhh. I don't have much time. I know Millie—she'll be back in here to fuss over you any second. Allow me to explain—"

Drawing a deep breath, Princess Amber closed her eyes

and scrunched up her brow as though she needed every ounce of concentration to say what she was about to say.

"The rumors that your father kidnapped me are true. He had found out about the betrayal of the snake people, and when his demands that Groq seek justice proved futile he thought he could harness my alchemical powers to restore balance in Glendoch. But I, being young, refused him."

Pain flickered across her face.

"So he struck a bargain with the snake people—trade my sister for me, and *he* would find them the tunnel they sought. He figured her sorcery would be as good as mine. The snake people agreed and, just like that, there I was—encased in fiery mud for the rest of my life for all I knew. But then my sister turned against him—got rid of him as soon as he had served her purpose."

Her expression darkened.

"Making it so easy for that fallen spirit to find her."

"You mean her wand?" Meylyne asked.

"Yes. It has a name—Thraxal—and is a story unto itself but we don't have time for that now. It was easy for Thraxal to prey upon Anastisse's bitterness. It promised her the revenge she sought and bit by bit it took the few traces of love she had left and bound them into this black opal."

Taking Meylyne's hand, she placed the black opal in her palm and closed Meylyne fingers around it.

"This is the second thing I needed to give you."

Another memory flashed into Meylyne's mind—her mother's face, twisted with hatred as she hissed, *"You're no daughter of mine."*

She dropped the opal on the bed. "I don't want it."

Princess Amber sighed.

"Meylyne, I know this is hard for you but I promise you that in her own flawed way your mother loved you very much." Her voice caught in her throat. "Perhaps she still does."

Meylyne snorted and Princess Amber snatched her wrists, holding them so tightly that it hurt.

"Listen, Meylyne, and listen well. You are a Rose, which means that you, too, have the potential to become a Thorn Queen. *All* we Roses do—so choose your thoughts and your actions wisely."

Princess Amber picked up the opal and put it back into Meylyne's hand. After a second's thought, Meylyne closed her fingers around it.

"How did you escape from the snake people?"

Standing up, Princess Amber moved to a window and pulled the drape aside. The air outside was violet. Meylyne guessed it was dusk.

"I didn't escape from them," Princess Amber answered. "They let me go. As soon as I found out that you were out looking for Prince Piam's cure I knew that you needed help to succeed, and succeed you must for Glendoch to endure. I told the snake people that *I* would guide you to the answer they sought, in return for which I wanted my freedom. They agreed, but insisted I assume the disguise of a snake until I had delivered on my promise."

Meylyne rolled the opal between her palms.

"And how did you have my Book of Incantations?"

"That is too long a story for right now. The short answer is that I found it. But it was always going to return to you. Anastisse was silly to think otherwise."

Meylyne held her gaze for a second, her mind roiling with questions. Then she shrugged. She had the right book now. Cradling the bowl of soup, she took a sip. It tasted bitter and sweet at the same time.

"So what now? Are you returning to the castle?"

Princess Amber shook her head. "Alas no, not yet. I must find your father."

Meylyne inhaled sharply and the hot liquid scorched her throat as it went down the wrong way. She coughed and spluttered, her bruised ribs exploding in agony. Princess Amber hurried back to her side and took the bowl of soup before it splashed all over the bed. After a few minutes the fit subsided and she lay back on her pillow, trying to draw air into lungs that felt like they'd been flattened beneath a pastry-roller.

"He's still alive?" she wheezed.

"I didn't say *that*."

Meylyne waited for Princess Amber to explain. Instead she placed her hands on Meylyne's shoulders and kissed the top of her head.

"Do not resist the role of Queen of Glendoch. It is rightfully yours and that for which you were born." Her eyes twinkled. "And you'll see—you'll have fun with it. Your friend Blue will live with you in the castle and your friends—Hope, Trin, Train, and Grimorex can visit whenever they like. All Glendoch's good is returning. I can feel it!"

As Princess Amber stood up, a pang of longing gripped Meylyne. She suddenly, and quite desperately, wanted her to stay.

"But what about you? Are you ever coming back?"

"Oh that I am. You can count on it."

With that, Princess Amber closed her eyes and Meylyne watched as her limbs melted back into her body and her skin became covered with scales. Once back in the form of a snake, she slithered over to the window and seconds later she was gone.

For a while Meylyne sat in the gloom, thinking about everything Princess Amber had said. Then a chink of light appeared in the room as the door opened a crack. Blue and Prince Piam tiptoed in.

"Nurse Millie is asleep outside," Prince Piam whispered, grinning.

"I thought you'd like some company," Blue added, crawling up into bed with her.

Meylyne could tell from the look in his eyes that he understood how she felt. After all—he'd been through it all with her. A warm flush of happiness spread through her and she squeezed his hand.

Prince Piam sat on the edge of the bed. Pointing at her hand he asked, "What's that?"

Meylyne looked down at the black opal shimmering black and green in the candlelight. "*That* is my mother's opal. And you will never believe who was just here . . ."

The End

ACKNOWLEDGMENTS

I started writing this book many years ago, before I owned a computer (this was back in the day when it was normal for a person not to own their own desktop computer, let alone laptop). It was a slow process. I would write up a few pages in my diary, take those pages into my office, type them up after work and save them to floppy disks. Needless to say, I've had a lot of help and input over the years! I am deeply grateful to the following people that have offered oodles of heartfelt help and support in one way or another;

My friends, Christine Elder, Georgina Kartsonis, Hilary Butler, Veronica Campbell, Miriam Sharland, Claire Haigh, Nisha Inalsingh, Jeanne Chung, Sarah Deroulade, Kim Forster, Denise Clover, Bettina Glenning, Natalia Kantor and Rebecca Leche. My critique group; Deborah Underwood, Rachel Rodriguez, Christie Andersen, Amy Trusso, Pat Nishita, and Heather Hughes. My illustrator; Elisabeth Alba. My editor, Stephen Roxburgh. The Plot Whisperer, Martha Alderson. The fearless team at She Writes Press/BookSparks; Brooke Warner, Samantha Strom, Elisabeth Kaufman and Crystal Patriache. My parents; Sylvia and Graham Holland and my brother, Seth Holland. And last but not least, my amazing husband, Kumar and my daughter, Isabel, who set my heart on fire with gratitude and love each and every day.

ABOUT THE AUTHOR

Photo credit: Emily Dulla

ELISE HOLLAND grew up in the English countryside, contentedly devouring the books of CS Lewis, Hans Christian Andersen, The Brothers Grimm and Enid Blyton before moving to Michigan in her early teens. While studying psychology at the University of Michigan, she developed a fascination for Jung, archetypes and the collective unconscious to which we all belong.

Now she lives in Mill Valley, CA, with her husband, daughter, dog, and cat. In addition to fueling her tea addiction, she enjoys hiking, yoga, and spending time with family and friends.

SELECTED TITLES FROM SPARKPRESS

The Blue Witch, Alane Adams, $16.95, 9781943006779. Nine-year-old Abigail Tarkana has a problem: her witch magic has finally come in, but it's *different*—and being different is a problem at the Tarkana Witch Academy. Together with her scientist-friend Hugo, she face off against sneevils, shreeks, and vikens in a race to discover the secrets about her mysterious magic.

But Not Forever, Jan Von Scleh, $16.95, 978-1-943006-58-8. When identical fifteen-year-old girls are mysteriously switched in time, they discover the love that's been missing in their lives. Torn, both want to go home, but neither wants to give up what they now have.

Serenade, Emily Kiebel. $15, 978-1-94071-604-6. After moving to Cape Cod after her father's death, Lorelei discovers her great-aunt and nieces are sirens, terrifying mythical creatures responsible for singing doomed sailors to their deaths. When she rescues a handsome sailor who was supposed to die at sea, the sirens vow that she must finish the job or faced grave consequences.

Red Sun, Alane Adams. $17, 978-1-940716-24-4. After learning that his mom is a witch and his missing father is a true Son of Odin, twelve-year-old Sam Baron must travel through a stonefire to the magical realm of Orkney on a quest to find his missing friends and stop an ancient curse.

Wendy Darling Vol 1: Stars, Colleen Oakes. $17, 978-1-94071-6-96-4. Loved by two men—a steady and handsome bookseller's son from London, and Peter Pan, a dashing and dangerous charmer—Wendy realizes that Neverland, like her heart, is a wild place, teeming with dark secrets and dangerous obsessions.

CPSIA information can be obtained
at www.ICGtesting.com
Printed in the USA
BVHW080529081218
535061BV00003B/6/P